THE ECHO OF SILENCE

A Chronicle of God, Creation, and the
Time Continuum

Alan E. Carman

Order this book online at www.trafford.com
or email orders@trafford.com

Most Trafford titles are also available at major online book retailers.

This is a work of fiction. All of the characters, names, incidents, organizations, and dialogue
in this novel are either the products of the author's imagination or are used fictitiously.

Printed in the United States of America.

ISBN: 978-1-4269-4101-6 (sc)
ISBN: 978-1-4269-4102-3 (hc)
ISBN: 978-1-4269-4103-0 (e)

Library of Congress Control Number: 2010916117

*Our mission is to efficiently provide the world's finest, most comprehensive book publishing
service, enabling every author to experience success. To find out how to publish your
book, your way, and have it available worldwide, visit us online at www.trafford.com*

Trafford rev. 10/30/2010

 www.trafford.com

North America & international
toll-free: 1 888 232 4444 (USA & Canada)
phone: 250 383 6864 ♦ fax: 812 355 4082

Contents

Preface

The Echo of Silence is a story of the covenant between God and time that made creation possible. The only person left alive on Earth in the year 2035 offers it to illuminate why human beings became an endangered species. His written testimony reveals the futility of the great controversy over creation between religion and science, a verbal conflict that has lasted more than four hundred years. The debate kept the world's populace off-balance and in a constant state of confusion and doubt over their origins.

The analogy of these conflicting beliefs was not conceived as a tribute or attempt to take sides in the debate. It describes the deplorable excesses of both factions who were responsible for the planet's demise. The two segments of society became the most powerful, influential, and dominant forces on Earth. Their reach extended into every aspect of the human experience, and the impact of these actions polarized the masses at a time when the world needed guidance and stability in order to survive.

It is not a pleasant or complimentary testimonial to mankind, for it exposes elements in our society that ignore God's mandates for living. There will be readers who will flinch at some of the unrepentant criticism of man. I can only suggest they open any newspaper or listen to any television news report to confirm the evaluation of the human life form. My story's main objective is a desire to bring closure to the great controversy between religion and science. With the current crisis over global warming, Earth's population lives in doubt and confusion over the future of mankind and his planet.

Although *The Echo Of Silence* is highly critical of the two most powerful influences on Earth, the author is not an academic, scientist, or theologian, only someone deeply concerned over a world in turmoil and man's irresponsible rush to self destruction. The earth's malaise centers on one specific question: how did man's undisciplined actions jeopardize the future of his planet? This story addresses the issue and is an in-depth analogy of God, creation, and the time continuum. Its range covers the birth of the universe, the origins of man, and his inept stewardship of our planet. Not a complimentary testimonial to the human life form. The debate, lasting four hundred years, was self defeating, as neither science nor religion could claim ownership of the genesis until they recognized the omnipotent nature and true function of the time continuum. A tragedy for mankind, as time is on God's side and not of God's creations.

As the author, I am neither a scientist nor a theologian and have no malice toward either party, only someone concerned with our planet's future. In my effort to include this idealism into the story, the often-repeated reference to mankind or man encompasses all of humanity: men, women, and children. There is no intent to slight or glorify either gender.

Elihu Proclaims God's Majesty to Job

He does great things, which we cannot comprehend.
For to the snow, he says, "Fall on Earth."—Job 37:5–6

By the breath of God, ice is given
and the broad waters are frozen fast.—Job 37:10

Whether for correction, or for his land, or for love,
he causes it to happen.—Job 37:13

The Beginning

In this terminal year of 2035, it is my belief that I am the last person left alive on our planet. Over the past thirty-five years, the continents and oceans have disappeared beneath an all-encompassing mantle of ice. The catastrophic events and causes, which led to the eradication of all life on Earth, defy explanation. At this late date my plight is hopeless, and I am resigned to my fate.

I began writing this story of our global crisis three months ago, after the demise of my three associate scientists. Because of the critical condition facing our world, we secluded ourselves in this nuclear power plant after our families perished. It eventually became our prison. My colleagues chose to end their lives with the DD 2030 capsule manufactured en masse before the pharmaceutical industry ceased operating. The doomsday pill provided a quick, painless death, preferred over starvation or freezing. I elected to bury my colleagues outside our facility in unfrozen ground.

Stationed around the plant's perimeter are four gigantic portable heat convectors that operate on power generated by our facility. They are positioned to face the four cardinal points of the compass. These huge concave discs radiate constant heat directly into the surrounding ice mass. The melted water is recycled to ensure the plant's continued operation. When fresh water became a scarce resource on Earth, these convectors were transported by seagoing tanker ships originally designed to carry oil, for these polar regions contained most of the world's fresh water. This lifesaving liquid was then carried back to major ports of entry to a thirsty populace.

The planet had experienced past glaciations, and various life forms had survived. These previous ice periods must now be considered trivial compared to the present chilling phenomenon, which has transformed our planet into an icy cocoon.

Outside, the extent of coldness is overwhelming. Were the scene not so deadly, the ice- covered landscape would be considered beautiful. Bathed in an eerie, unearthly blue light, the vision chills the very soul. As our planet orbits the sun, its brilliance is somewhat obscured, and the overhead sky is subjected to interchanging oddities of color. At night, fantastic wavering curtains of flickering lights, ghostly veils, and shrieking winds never cease, along with the deafening reverberations from the expanding ice, a constant reminder of my fate.

As all things must eventually end, I cannot delay the inevitable. The master computer has registered a red warning light. This indicates that the fissionable nuclei will be exhausted in three days. When this happens, my power source will be terminated. I will then be at the mercy of the encroaching ice. I have finished my narrative, knowing full well that no one will ever read its contents. It was a combined effort to relate my beliefs with a consensus among my former associates. We unanimously agreed on the main causes responsible for our planet's demise.

My mission in writing this paper was to illuminate the destructive factions in our global society that resulted in this disaster, as well as the planet's two most powerful influences over mankind's thoughts and actions failing to ensure its future.

Faced with our current situation, it is obvious the annihilating forces were already here on Earth, in the form of man. It is ironic that throughout these last terminal years, the prediction of the doomsday prophecy was to be from destructive forces from space.

This is the final episode in the story of humanity. It stands as a reluctant and sad testimonial to the duplicity of the human race for desecrating our sanctuary in the universe. An irresponsible tragedy severed the covenant between God and his chosen people. My last act will be to post this chronicle in a time capsule. Perhaps in some distant future, another form of life will visit our planet and discover what transpired. For now, I will simply deed it to the archives of infinity.

The following is the tragic story of the degeneration of mankind and the demise of his planet.

The Genesis Age

Between ten and twenty billion years ago, before the universe existed, the consecrated sanctuary for all that was to be was the hallowed void of space. It lingered as a frigid state of obscurity, confined to an indefinite age of darkness. This endless realm hosted only two invisible forces. One was a supreme deity who would be recognized as God, the exalted source of creation. The act of creating had one constraint: the creator could not function without the aid of time, the other invisible force. This medium was a perpetual conduit that transformed the creator's aspirations into reality. With no beginning or ending, both were omnipotent and synonymous with creation. Their mutual bond was a covenant that would outlast eternity.

Evolving over eons, the age of darkness was in a transitional state, separating the collapse of a previous universe and the birth of a new one. As space existed in a benign state, it lacked meaning or purpose. By divine revelation, the creator visualized a change that would counteract the gloomy stigma of endless darkness—the desire to evoke his will and lift the self-imposed moratorium on the indefinite age of darkness.

Utilizing the dust and matter from the previous universe, the creator molded and surrendered his embodiment into a gigantic swirling mass. In so doing, he committed his spiritual being into the sphere.

This divine gift assured that everything manifested would contain his spirituality. The revolving mass loomed as an embryonic seed implanted in the womb of space.

God's will could not be restrained, and suddenly an explosion of tremendous magnitude convulsed the very heart of space. A fracture appeared in the curtain of darkness, and from its folds blossomed a fantastic corsage of ever-changing color and light. The brilliance spread outward to illuminate the dark reaches of the void. This was the birth of a new universe. It would be called the "genesis."

From this inferno and energy generated by the cataclysmic explosion, chemistry had come into play. Glowing matter was flung outward to shower space. These huge glowing formations appeared as sparkling jewels decorating the heavens. It caused a cosmic chain reaction as star building seeded the nebulous horizons of the void. This was God's firmament and the beginning of a new age.

Over millions of years, there was no end to the evolving universe. As it expanded, galaxies formed to array themselves with millions of star clusters. The celestial islands, each with suns and moons and organized by the force of gravity became sparkling panoramas. This vast transformation of cosmic bodies continued for millions of years. Many generations of older stars exhibited vigorous tendencies, only to exhaust their fiery furnaces. They simply exploded in violent disarray and succumbed to the chilling vacuum of space. Many that remained intact were bombarded by lethal space debris.

The creator's scarred planets and moons became cosmic graveyards, the first entries into the fossil records, remaining as permanent evidence of God's creativity. The termination of these heavenly bodies set a precedent for all creation that followed. Everything God created would know a limited existence with birth, life, and death. The creator commemorated a new age of refinement with the birthing of this new universe.

Millions of years after the genesis, a spherical halo of two hundred thousand billion stars, glowing nebulae, had evolved in space.

Along the outer edges of this milky-appearing galaxy space dust accumulated, forming a new solar system. In this constantly expanding universe, the forces of gravity within the dust cloud forced it to collapse into a flat, revolving disc and then into a contracting center surrounded by a series of concentric rings. They contained an aggregate of dust and gases, each destined to hold a definite position in the newly forming solar system. Throughout the succeeding years, the heaviest elements sank within massive cores, each with an atmosphere enveloped by light gases. The center of the formation contained most of the original dust cloud and was cold and incandescent. Eventually this mass constricted to critical density, and nuclear reactions within the interior began to generate heat, giving birth to a new sun.

The concentric rings around the sun condensed and became planets, each positioned to form a new solar system. As time worked its magic, the solar radiation boiled away the masses, and what remained were the warm, shrunken inner planets and gaseous outer planets. Finally, this cosmic newcomer completed its evolutionary stages of development and filled a void in the parent galaxy. The final composition contained one star (the sun), nine planets, and their thirty-one satellite moons, thousands of asteroids, and billions of comets. God then selected the third planet from the sun, which would become known as Earth, to perform the miracle that would bring fulfillment to his divinity.

In its early stages of development, Earth reacted violently against the forces that had delivered it into the universe. It exhibited all of the tendencies of a newborn infant throwing a tantrum. In this primordial setting, the planet emerged as a solid landmass with vast plains and deep, gaping depressions. The entire surface was divided into ten crystal plates, subdivided into various sizes. These tectonic plates floated on the inner molten core one hundred miles below the surface. Hot magnum and gaseous currents on the underside of the plates caused them to move. When they collided, earthquakes occurred and the floors of the oceans split open, allowing molten lava to appear where none had existed before. The sea floors expanded, mountain ranges were thrust upward, and the landmasses experienced continental drift.

This re-shifting and recycling of the earth's exterior crust made for a catastrophic world. Eventually the original landmass divided into four different continents and then drifted apart at the rate of one inch per year. When this continental disbursement occurred, everything on the surface was transported into new temperate zones. In the years to come, this condition had devastating effects on all evolving life on Earth. The monstrous age of dinosaurs knew two continents during their one hundred fifty-million-year reign on Earth. The succeeding age of mammals knew at least eight fragmented continents as their homeland. Widespread extinctions of many species occurred when tropical environments were transported into milder zones. The extinction of life forms from continental drift also became part of Earth's fossil record.

During these transitional periods, vegetation died, settled, and became leaf beds for plant life. The rotted foliage turned into peat with a mixture of sand and mud. The pressure of water compressed the mixture, and the buckling of Earth wrought tremendous pressure, which formed coal. Much of the same process formed huge subterranean deposits of oil and gas. These fossil fuels were a divine legacy left in the earth for a future life form's survival, precious resources that should not be squandered, for they were not renewable.

As the landscape of Earth developed, it was one of desolation. The lowland areas were obscured by cloud cover so dense that sunlight could not penetrate the layers. The internal pressure from within the earth's molten core forced fiery ash and gas fumes through the vents of the crust. In the neo-darkness setting, time provided the miracle the creator had envisioned, a transformation of inorganic matter to organic. Molecules began to multiply, first as single cells and then into clusters of soft cells. These early forms were the first signs of life on Earth and became the basic organic seeds for every form of life to appear on the planet. In order for these organisms to grow and multiply, they needed nourishment, and it would be derived from a competitive world where each creature preyed on the other in order to survive.

Over millions of years the Earth's surface cooled and water vapor condensed into clouds. As they accumulated, condensation fell back to Earth as rain. Over long periods, the spattering became a deluge, and water filled the lowland basins, becoming the first shallow seas. When they eventually expanded in depth, they became the oceans of the world and covered 70 percent of its surface. The water lapped against the higher land obstructions that formed the other 30 percent of the planet's surface. As the cloud cover dissipated, sunlight caressed the land and seas with stimulating rays of warmth.

Far below the sunlit waters of the saline cradles was a new stirring among microorganisms. Fantastic new divisions of cells occurred, and reproductions emerged as new life forms. As each appeared, they were introduced to a combative and hostile world. The explosion of new life turned the secluded underwater domain into an aquatic wonderland, with exquisite fungi and algae wavering among gentle ocean currents. Soft jellyfish floated ponderously, and small trilobites scuttled across the ocean floor. Many bizarre forms appeared and were baptized in the great sea of life.

Throughout the initial stages of creation was a tendency to overpopulate the oceans with millions of new species, and there was not enough room or food to support their existence. The competitive situation caused survival to be critical. Domains of safety were established for all living creatures that had become combatants, and in order to coexist, the strong preyed on the weak.

In this dangerous setting, the creator recognized the need to regulate his creations' defenses. He introduced camouflage, protective coloration, repulsive tastes, nauseating odors, mimicry, and mummery, establishing a less combative playing field. Survival of the fittest became survivor of the craftiest and most artful. The more favorable variants the creatures had, the more their edge to survive increased. Those life forms that adapted to the stresses of their environment lived and multiplied. Those that could not simply perished and became part of the fossil record.

When the first amphibious creatures escaped from their water bondage, they stepped forth into a changing world. The land, once a primordial, barren, and desolate landscape had been transformed into an exotic paradise. Lush vegetation blanketed the surface with jungles, shaded pools, endless forests, and savannahs, all with reservoirs of fresh water. This embellishment of Earth, which the creator had decreed, was only made possible by time.

The new land dwellers soon experienced the same hostile and combative world as their predecessors beneath the sea. With time as the medium for change, the creator brought forth a diversity of new life forms that reproduced millions of evolving species. These varied forms ranged from invertebrates to fish to amphibians to reptiles to birds. Countless legions inundated all realms of Earth, from ocean depths to land beneath its surface, to sky and shimmering deserts, to steaming jungles, the plains, and the highest mountains.

Then the magnificent paradise on Earth God had envisioned became a utopia. Through God all life would proliferate and spread their species over the land and under the sun. Eventually, as new life appeared, they crossed continents and entered new hemispheres, claiming their rite of passage. Their global sanctuary was one of mind-stunning beauty, truly heaven on earth. Every visible thing was enriched with the creator's essence. His spiritual embellishment personified all of creation. In the future, this earthly setting would become the proving grounds for his greatest accomplishment. It was only a matter of time.

The Age of Mankind

Over the millennium, the creator filled the earth to overflowing with multitudes of diverse life forms. They appeared in many shapes and sizes. Some were huge, ferocious, cumbersome, and grotesque, supporting tiny brains. The one hundred and sixty-five-million-year reign of the dinosaurs produced the most terrifying creatures to ever roam the earth. Even with this diversity of life, God found no satisfaction in creation for the sake of creating. It had become a redundant process without purpose or objective. What was served by repetitious creation? No emerging species had the ability to recognize and acknowledge God. In itself, the practice had become meaningless, just a recurring enigma.

Thus by divine revelation, God saw the need for change through an age of refinement. He would introduce a new species with special perceptive features that would assure recognition of his divinity. In determining the various characteristics of this newcomer, he did not visualize a similarity to any other previous life form. His past creations lacked the physical dexterity and mental capabilities to become a superior life form. His visionary concept was not of a colossus but of an ordinary profile. He would not fly, crawl, slither, or crouch but would walk upright. For a prototype of this unique life form he would select a species already actively in place. This abrupt departure from traditional acts of creation would set a precedent and be recognized as "selective creation." It was a divine effort to bring creation into perspective by eliminating the mundane order and changeless rhythms of creating.

By divine revelation and intervention, God chose to anoint the primate order since they were the predominant intelligence on Earth and possessed a unique physical bearing. When this prototype matured, he would shed his cloak of bestiality. As his mental capacity developed, inborn animal instincts would wane but never completely disappear. Eventually this newcomer would acquire seven distinct qualities that would separate him from the animal: love, tenderness, mercy, tolerance, patience, consideration, and compassion. It would then be recognized as a human being. As humans were created in God's image, these humanitarian qualities emulated the creator's persona. They would establish man's reputation as a repetition of the creator and fortify him to face any obstacle and deal with life's adversities.

As primitive man struggled to gain a foothold on Earth and walk upright, his physical appearance changed notably. The original handicaps of primates were restricted to moving in a perpetual crouch. They sometimes reared upright but were unable to extend their legs and were therefore forced to stand on the soles of their feet. When they became bipedal, the primates no longer needed long arms for support. Their feet had large and small toes instead of clumsy claws or hooves, which increased their range of vision through increased height, and he could then spot the approach of a distant enemy. The process of physical development also provided a main arch reaching from the heel bone to the ball of the foot. This advantage prevented shocks or jars to the spinal column. In this upright position his torso was short, with legs longer than his arms for balance. To support this posture, his spine had a double curve rather than a single one. His prognathous facial profile—with its massive projecting jaw—set him apart from the anthropoids. Sparse body hair instead of a full coat of fur further enhanced and defined his human appearance.

Like all previous life forms, human beings were exposed to a combative world where the strong survived and the weak perished. In this hostile situation, more aggressive adversaries would be able to overcome him in physical combat. His most advantageous asset was his enlarged brain. His ability to think and reason more than compensated for his lack of physical strength. He could outthink and outmaneuver—but not outdistance—some of his rivals. Most living creatures shunned his approach, for they sensed his physical appearance as a threat. Their instincts were well founded, for once he had a weapon in his hand, man became one of the most formidable predators on Earth.

Along with his newly acquired superiority came responsibility, but this did not materialize for thousands of years. How man learned to handle this burden would shape his mental outlook on life and would decide his species' future.

The process of selective creation, although conclusive, had one unavoidable handicap. God, in his infinite wisdom to create miracles, could not do so without time. He was completely dependent on this medium to carry out his wishes and make creation a reality.

With a desire to begin the birthing of his new life form, the creator selected the garden spot, the Dark Continent, for the birthplace of mankind; this was the hereditary homeland of the primates. Situated against a backdrop of broad plains, savannahs, and green forests, this utopia contained all the natural resources necessary for man's survival.

The lineup of primitive actors who would appear on the world stage had no earthly peers. When the curtain of time was parted, the play itself would have no equal plot. As the spellbinding drama unfolded, it would fascinate the assembly. Ironically, after the final curtain call, there would be no acclamations from the audience, only stunned disbelief, so impressive was the birth of man.

The creator had decreed that most living creatures would be equipped with sensory organs similar to men. They had the same ability to see, hear, smell, taste, and touch. Man inherited the same qualities, with one exception. His brain was capable of retaining experiences and then storing them in his memory banks. Because he had the ability to communicate by speech, these experiences were passed on over generations. This accumulated knowledge gave mankind an absolute edge over all living creatures on Earth.

As human beings were of a sensitive nature, their vibrancy of mind allowed them to experience pain, suffering, despair, hate, love, compassion, indifference, joy, and happiness. Although these emotions were complementary, there was a downside to this area of expression. All creatures, including man, shared an inborn hostility, suspicion, and combativeness toward each other. For most species, this aggressive behavior was motivated by the need to survive. Thousands of years in the future, this instinct would wane and be channeled into a more subtle approach utilized by man. It would be expressed in religious and racial bigotry and would expose a distinct flaw in man's character.

The duel quality of thought conveyance had no parallel in other life forms. Man's voice would be raised on many occasions for numerous reasons. This would prove to be insignificant compared to acknowledging God and singing his praises.

One of the most expressive characteristics of humans would be their hands. Not only were they sensitive but versatile, permitting him to perform a variety of feats. Man could use them to dig, feed himself, swim, crawl, sign language, write, cook, fight, and express love. When he reached mental maturity, his gifted use would be folding them together in prayer. By this gesture he would formally accept God as his savior. This acknowledgement was the chosen creation's purpose in life, his manifest destiny.

As the world God created became a competitive and combative hunting preserve, man would be forced to adopt and find a secure future to survive. How would humans fare in this hostile environment? God gave man free will to decide his own destiny. It was an awesome responsibility. The choices and decisions he made would determine the future of his species and planet.

As these prototypes of early humans eventually ventured forth from living in trees to walk upright and find shelter in caves, an evolutionary division occurred in their physical appearance. New branches of life emerged with a role call emulating out of antiquity, from Sivapithecus to Australopithecus to Homo erectus, to neanderthal, and finally to Homo sapiens. The beautiful world God had prepared for man stretched from ocean to ocean and from mountains to vast plains.

Man's precarious journey through life would take him across the sweep of continents, always curious about what lay beyond the next horizon. As the geological features of Earth were transformed by catastrophic events, he found himself constantly adopting new methods of foraging and adapting to different lifestyles. Finally, after leaving his footprints across continents, man migrated into the Western hemisphere. Now the human dynasty on Earth was worldwide. Over centuries, wherever man trod, he left physical evidence of his passing hidden in multi-levels on Earth. Each successive generation left remnants of its culture. These manmade fossils verified man's rite of passage.

As man evolved, he learned innovative skills and adopted natural resources for fashioning tools and weapons. He came of age when he learned how to control fire for cooking and warmth. Finally the noble human stood with his feet planted firmly on the ground. His free-swinging arms radiated self-confidence and aided him in new methods of defense, as well as assisted in attacks on his adversaries. His unique appearance and actions altered the complexity of life on Earth, for he would challenge every living thing for supremacy. The obstacles he encountered tested his courage and tenacity. If he preserved his human dignities and human qualities, he would experience a brief spiritual relationship with God. This mutual bond would ultimately ensure his eventual salvation and an afterlife with his creator.

Any success in obtaining his spiritualism would take its toll on man's superior intellect. This divine grant set him apart from less-gifted creatures on Earth. How he made use of this precious asset would be his foremost achievement. Incredibly, his ascent from primates evolved into the most dominant life form on the planet. His one handicap was the absence of divine oversight of his thought and reasoning powers. This missing link with God left him vulnerable to life's temptations. It made the human race responsible for its own actions.

The human brain was like a delicate scale. The weight of intolerable strain and personal problems could tip the balance one way or the other. Man's only secure direction in life was to maintain a stable balance and recognize good from bad and right from wrong. These standards would be acquired by his upbringing, family life, education, church, and personal contract with others. To assist his mental outlook and earthly actions he would be exposed to spiritual guidelines governing human morality and behavior. Mankind's future and the welfare of his planet loomed as a huge question mark. If he could not cope with his mental overload, the tenure of his journey through life would be short-lived.

As gifted as man's capabilities were, they had one restraint. He could only process one problem at a time; handling more than one produced a strain on his mental reserves. In the future, this dilemma would affect his development. The overburden of stress could overwhelm his sensibilities. For all of man's gifted qualifications as a unique species, the human race concealed a hidden burden buried deep in its inner conscience. The primordial instincts from his animal ancestry would always remain an intricate part of his makeup. If the burden of life's problems became unbearable and effect his mental progression, a regression of the evolutionary process would occur. The obvious trigger for this emotional upheaval would stem from the overburdening of personal and worldly problems.

God's commitment to mankind required God to achieve a pinnacle of perfection in a given time. This would allow man to grow in stature and mentally and physically assume leadership of the planet.

It would be man's greatest challenge, and with a limited life cycle, there was no room for failure.

What would the future hold for the human race? Would man walk upright in a straight line, with his head held high, or in circles, always looking down?

God's choice of selective creation was not without ramifications. Over time it would test the complexity of evolution. The continuous process of transformation had been constant and undisturbed throughout the ages. The birth of man broke its continuity. The conception of man was the most radical and momentous undertaking implemented by the creator. It set a precedent by conceiving a life form and tailoring it to God's specifications for an explicit purpose. No previous life form on Earth had been empowered with special perceptive capabilities. Human beings were created in God's image. They were expected to acquire the seven humanitarian qualities that defined God's divinity. His gift of life was a mutual spiritual contract, as if to say, "Believe in me and I will give you eternal life." He established man's lifecycle on that premise.

God laid down four markers for man's lifecycle. Three were definite: birth, life, and death. The fourth was arbitrary and wholly dependent on his embracing of God. If achieved, this fourth marker was his passport to an eternal afterlife. The contract between God and man resembled a triangle, a polygon exhibiting three plains. The lines started at birth, and then up to the pinnacle of life, back down to the transition of death, and then returned to the starting point with an afterlife. It was the creator's eternal triangle and man would be its only recipient.

Human life expectancy was eighty-six years. Many people would prefer that life was a never-ending story, but time decided otherwise. Many are seduced by this dream, which is part of expectation and hope, but it is also a time to face reality. With a fading lifespan, people began to lose their memories, which seemed to dissolve into a blurred haze of obscurity. Man was then forced to ask the question: Was my life a happy and joyful experience? Was it a complete failure?

The answer was buried deep in his unconscious. It was only attainable if he achieved his manifest destiny.

Although man had no rival with a superior intelligence, all other earthly life forms held a distinct advantage over him. Except for the threat of predators, they would live a natural, carefree existence far removed from the debilitating pressure of personal and worldly affairs. However, humans were different. They would create and live in a pressure-cooker society with untold manmade hardships, obstacles, and problems. Eventually, this crushing burden would force people to their knees. At this moment in his life, when his responsibilities became unbearable, he would look to the heavens for divine guidance and salvation. There was no greater joy than to surrender one's heart, body, and soul to God. In the future, would God's faith and commitment to mankind be justified? Only time would tell.

With the early development of mankind resolved, his progression entered a new phase by expanding his knowledge of the planet he inhabited. To some people, evolution is a stretch of the imagination. Yet its application is not restricted to life forms but includes everything God created. Even civilizations would rise to great heights, only to decline and disappear. But new ones rose from the ashes and resulted in greater prominence. By this process, everything that perished left a permanent record of its passing, preserved by time. This is not accidental but God's way of leaving proof of his divinity.

As man's knowledge of his planet grew, so did his need for resources. In time vast armadas of ships and crews crisscrossed the oceans of the world for those resources, as well as for trade and to acquire wealth. This called for complex accounting systems, and mathematics and writing came into being. Education flourished, teaching young and old the history of Earth. Courts grew into cities and eventually nations. Specialists became artisans and science found its footing. Priests, scientists, and astronomers began to study and plot the movement of the heavenly bodies. The most learned and intelligent became scholars, offering philosophical theories and inventions.

These were the dedicated factions of earthen society who laid the foundation of religion and science.

In the distant future, the issue of the past and present source of creation would challenge and perplex the most brilliant minds. They would engage in endless debates over its sponsorship, never acknowledging that time was the active conduit that carried out God's will. Both God and time cosponsored the birth of the universe. It was never the act of one force. Their combined power dominates the universe with their presence. When man eventually contemplates eternity, he will find that God and time are its only occupants.

The Great Controversy

After man crossed over the threshold of life, he faced the daunting task of establishing an appropriate code of conduct to live by. His long evolutionary journey had taken its toll. Many pitfalls and obstacles challenged his thoughts and reasoning powers. As Gods' selected creation, humans were being tested every moment and accepted the challenge as their rite of passage .Throughout the early stages of man's development, the world around him became a never-ending curiosity. He pondered his origins. Who was he? where had he come from? and what was his purpose in life?

As time worked its revolutionary magic, humans emerged as the dominant life form. In spite of his elevated status, man was insecure, always retaining a basic feeling of inadequacy and fear of the unknown. This handicap became his foremost nemesis. His concerns were numerous: earthquakes, hurricanes, typhoons, tornadoes, floods, droughts, tidal waves, and bombardment of Earth by lethal space debris. These natural disasters reminded him of his insecurity and mortality. Above all else, he had a morbid fear of death. After many years of soul-searching for mental security, it became obvious that he needed faith in someone or something.

Over the millennia he realized his deliverer did not exist on Earth. This unknown entity could only be someone who gave him life and a planet to live out his time on Earth. This supreme entity would be known as God. The gift of life granted man was not without a reciprocal responsibility to the creator. Man was required to acknowledge his benefactor with love and devotion. This obligation was man's destiny. As years turned into centuries, his spiritual awakening was slow to mature. Early on, his search for a divine attachment was languished on heavenly bodies such as the sun and moon as symbols to worship. He even adopted animals and created stone idols. Eventually, these unresponsive physical manifestations lost their significance and were abandoned.

In desperation for guidance and a solution to his dilemma, he sought help from within the world community. Two prominent but opposing factions surfaced to offer conflicting visions and beliefs on creation and man's origins. One was the religious community, whose beliefs were based on ancient holy scriptures written by man. The other was the scientific establishment advocating creation as a natural working of universal chemistry. These two professional combatants inherited the responsibility of verifying man's beginnings and his place in the universe. Clarification was decidedly in favor of science. Theologians' only "proof" of their beliefs were the man-written accounts of creation in their holy scriptures. Scientific inquiry was invested in deciphering the fossil record of heaven and Earth. Here in the dusty archives of Earth and the cold reaches of space lay the entire physical history of creation preserved by time. Whereas the religious faction had no physical evidence to prove their case, scientific beliefs were based on hard physical evidence. Their code of conduct was centered on the premise of "seeing is believing." The outcome of their arguments presented a physical chronology of creation preserved by the time continuum. This invisible frontier, preempted the past, hosted the present, and would be the unending sequel to the future.

The downside of the controversy between the two factions was a debate that lasted more than four hundred years. Its controversial issues kept the world's masses in a constant state of confusion and doubt. The verbal tug of war became a major distraction for mankind.

Confirming his origins and birth of the universe were the hallmark for survival of the human species.

From the first moment God anointed man with life, he was under a divine microscope to justify his rite of passage. As a selected species, humans were the only life form with the mental capacity to recognize its creator. This unique characteristic also allowed humans to acquire the seven qualities that separated them from their animal ancestry (as mentioned before: love, tenderness, thoughtfulness, mercy, decency, tolerance, and consideration for others). Without these human qualities, man would never rise above his kinship with other animals.

As the creator exercised no control or influence over man's thoughts, impulses, or judgments, man's actions were of his own, deciding life's decisions. The greatest challenge was to marshal his mental facilities to the point of self reliance. People were pressed every moment to fortify their mental reserves against outside elements of society that could lead them astray. Their defensive efforts were a never-ending process to maintain mental stability without divine oversight. Man's ultimate goal was to develop a strong moral resistance to destructive influences and to concentrate on achieving the seven qualities that identified the human race. Undoubtedly, human beings were the most unpredictable and complex life form ever created. His mood swings, thought processes, and subsequent actions were sometimes ungovernable and reckless. He had never mastered self analysis and mind control. Without question, if God had any influence over man's mental judgments, there would never have been wars, crime, drugs, greed, or any of the vices that dehumanized his special creation. Man's paramount responsibility was the intelligent stewardship of preserving his sanctuary in the universe.

In his continual search for a secure and peaceful life, there were no guarantees. He faced many trials and tribulations that tested his courage and resolve. Human beings aspired to rise above their status as a common life form. They met life's challenges with courage and conviction and a lifetime of hard labor. Recognition of man's achievements inflated his ego and self-esteem. Moments of glory where rare, but when they occurred, his spiritual being soared like an eagle high above the earth to rejoice and bond with his creator. Eventually, after many failures, man's decision-making process became a series of trial and error. This mental deficiency was normal in the progression of a new species without divine intervention over his actions. In reality, intrusive and persuasive parties could influence their thoughts and actions to their particular agendas. This friendly persuasion was sometimes unreliable, false, or deceptive and could complicate his journey through life. All above all other considerations, he had to accept the impact time would have on his decision making.

The creator's priceless gift of mental superiority to man was untested and immature at birth. By utilizing time, God would hone and temper his mental progress to achieve spiritual purity by adopting a golden rule: "Do unto others as you would have them do unto you." This humble guideline was the key to an emotionally pure and bountiful life. However these joyful rewards were under the relentless restrictions of time. Man could ill afford to misuse or squander one precious moment of its passing. A misguided course in life, marked by unwise decisions, brought sorrow, despair, and mental anguish. Wise decisions offered a rich life filled with peace and tranquility. The latter was only attainable by spiritual enlightenment.

Man's trials and ordeals began at birth and only end when completing his lifecycle. The earliest parts of his infant and childhood years were filled with wonder, bewilderment, and curiosity. They were followed by learning and decision making, to prepare for a responsible future. After adolescence there was a lengthy attempt to establish guidelines and moral standards to live by, which were often determined by his upbringing, parents, church, and life experiences. For families who lost loved ones to illness, aging, accidents, or natural causes, there was little relief from heartbreaking sorrow. This was the moment when humans sought divine salvation. Only God and time were the ultimate healers and could relieve their mental anguish.

Time acted as a two-edged sword. During man's early years, as he struggled to cope with life's complexities, time was his best friend, but its passing could be his worst enemy. All bodily functions tended to decline with aging. It is God's way of telling man he has a limited time to realize his destiny. There were other trying moments associated with growing old, such as when elders reached the apex of life and life sometimes became redundant. It became a reality that there were few earthly pleasures or challenges that had not been experienced. There was little time left for regrets, forming memories, or the luxury of bonding with the creator before his time ran out.

When people pass midlife, time seems to accelerate; days, months, and years slip by in quick succession. This is the moment to be thankful that God has granted a before-life and the promise of an afterlife. That final union with God is the most fulfilling experience of one's life. It dissolves all past disappointments, sorrows, and unpleasant memories.

When reviewing man's past difficulties, and the conflicting viewpoints between religion and science, there was a glaring disparity. Both conceded that the birth of the universe was not a random act but was likely conducted by something or someone. Scientists contend that the event was a natural phenomena caused by a source they are as yet incapable of labeling. This vague and uncertain position left broad latitude for speculation, especially in a profession so rigidly structured. In spite of their opposing viewpoints, there were clues and facts that could settle the issue. The unknown source of creation was an unsatisfactory way of living in ignorance of one's beginnings. If the founder of creation was not identified, the physical universe and man's role as a life form would always remain an unexplained phenomena. When science labored to unlock the mystery of universal creation, they were hindered by a misguided concept of time. They insisted that time was not active prior to genesis. Its birthing coincided with the explosive act called the Big Bang Theory.

It is inconceivable that the only two entities in the age of darkness were inactive and unproductive for thousands of years. God and time required extensive preparation to formulate and then expedite creation. Their combined actions were infinite and not subjected to inactivity. The vast and empty vacuum of space identified the dark period. Where did the trace elements of matter come from? What force molded and formed them into a dense mass to become a nucleolus for the initial explosion? Without the active participation of time, neither God nor interacting chemistry could have orchestrated the genesis. Science cannot ignore that time is infinite, and so is God. They act in concert as one and are inseparable. These two life forces are responsible for creation and are the source scientists cannot label by scientific description. The origin of the unexplained matter circulating in space were the remnants of a previously collapsed or imploded universe. Universe proliferation was a reoccurring process, as ageless as God and time, and is the hallmark of their creative achievements.

The science of interacting chemistry also results in change but has no motivation or purpose and certainly no alliance with time. In comparing the longevity of religion and science, in comparing the appearance of religion and applied science the latter was a late arrival, whereas religion has endured for more than two thousand years. Science was a late arrival, but its impact fueled the rise of civilization on Earth. When the biblical account of creation was written, the word *science* was not even in man's vocabulary. This field of human endeavor appeared fourteen hundred years later, in the 1600s. In its early stage, curious individuals of vision began experimenting and testing theories relating to matter and alchemy. This was the earliest form of chemistry, dealing with metal workings, medicine, and other crafts. The development of chemical manufacturing began in the 1700s. Only then did early pioneers lay the groundwork for the science of modern chemistry. As their discoveries and efforts flourished, organic and inorganic chemistry became the wave of the future for the industrial world.

For scientists to justify their opposing positions against religious accountability, one discrepancy is apparent. Scientific appraisal of religion as a faith-based society is somewhat hypercritical because so is their profession. Both embrace an invisible force; one accepts God, the other time. This discounts the scientific conviction that "seeing is believing." Incredibly, both parties ignore and cannot realize that time is a powerhouse that drives the universe. No one has ever identified the actual function of time. To further complicate the creation issue, man's understanding the science of physics was not complete and was hard to fathom. Scientists' greatest error was classifying the genesis as a natural event or accidental phenomenon without a sponsor. Ironically, acknowledging a divine origin for the birthing act did not disqualify or demean their professional standing. The workings of science were comparable to those of time, but without this medium, science was dysfunctional. Why is it so difficult for one profession to make concessions to another when facts speak for themselves? In identifying the creation process itself, there is one fictional aspect of the birthing act that both religion and science needed to address: a belief that instantaneous creation is possible when it is not. In spite of the miraculous achievements accredited to God, he could not wave a magic wand and make life forms or the universe instantly materialize. This creative capability was not possessed by God, time, or interacting chemistry. In confirming the limitations of the creator, it is necessary to refer to the before and after birthing of the universe, as well as the nine-month birth of God's only son, Jesus Christ.

At the center of the debate over the source of creation, another fact has to be considered. What purpose or satisfaction did God hope to gain by repetitious creation, for the sake of creating? He introduced billions of life forms over astronomical periods of time. The abrupt appearance of the human species represented a complete departure from God's traditional method of creating. The event of man was unquestionably the result of "selective creation."

Man was the only life form to ever be endowed with special perceptive features, making him capable of recognizing and acknowledging his benefactor. Over time God's creative efforts had become redundant, an exercise in futility without divine recognition. If man had not appeared on the world stage, creation would always remain in limbo. Neither God nor the universe would ever have been acknowledged. For the first time in the annals of creation, human beings brought meaning and purpose to God's efforts. This was the beginning of his grand design. The alternative was an anomaly, a universe unrecognized and harboring past generations of expired planets, one monumental cosmic graveyard with no attendant.

Because of the perpetual momentum of time, once set in motion, it could not be restrained or stopped. This was evident in the formula of God's grand design, blanketing the earth with unending multitudes of life forms. Their presence was visible in every realm of the planet. Subsequent generations transformed Earth into a colossal proving ground for his creativity. The preponderance of new life was destined to experience incredible hardships and devastating natural disasters. These reoccurring catastrophic events would rearrange the planet's surface and cause a tragic loss of life. Tectonic plate dispersal and the bombardment of Earth with lethal space debris brought mass extinctions. In spite of these horrendous casualties, the chain of life remained unbroken, a testimonial to the power of God and time.

To understand science's role in creation, it was imperative that we review its beginnings. Of all the life forms to appear on Earth, man was the most curious. From the very first moment of his deliverance, he beheld the breathtaking beauty of his world. The stark splendor of the heavens provided a kaleidoscope of the past. The endless panorama of heavenly lights overhead not only offered a glimpse of space but the history and progression of creation unfolding before his eyes, a scene that unquestionably linked God's presence with millions of years dedicated to universe building. Man saw light emanating from distant galaxies that had taken billions of years to reach his eyes. Even for suns that no longer existed, their afterglow lingered in space. Man's insatiable curiosity about his surroundings never ceased and eventually led to the birth of science.

In 1965, two scientists using sophisticated electronic equipment identified noise made by background radiation still circulating the vastness of space. What they confirmed was the preserved and continuous reverberations left over from the birth of the universe, a monumental discovery that confirmed God's relationship with time.

Due to the flexibility of man's nature, the natural world he inherited was never adequate to fulfill his needs for living. He was never content with the utopian paradise God had provided. He set out to rearrange and alter its appearance to suit his needs, to control or adjust the conditions he faced in life. But there was one unseen problem with his undertaking: the nurturing and renewal of life to preserve his planet depended on God's influence over time, a luxury man did not share. For humans to tamper with God's grand design broke a tradition that had existed four million years and was self defeating. In his rush to utilize time, he invented technological innovations that allowed him to adjust his room and water temperatures, and this breakthrough permitted him to live in any climate or environment on Earth. Not content to walk through life, again technology allowed him to fly and even gain excess to space. All of these scientific marvels satisfied his lust for life, but there was a limit to self gratification, and it had a way of ruling one's life.

To navigate the future, man would be forced to tread a precarious balancing act to maintain intelligent stewardship of his planet. The earth could not sustain repeated assaults to its surface and indiscriminate depletion of its underground resources, which took millions of years to form and were not renewable. Without sound and intelligent management, man and his home planet's future would be in jeopardy.

In spite of the wonderful accomplishments of science, they were overshadowed by irresponsible actions. Each industrial plant that produced an endless flow of commercial products to enrich man's life also released tons of pollution from burning fossil fuels into the earth's atmosphere. This cycle of irresponsibility left unchecked was a recipe for disaster. The contamination began with the industrial revolution in the1800s and continued unabated to the present. With every new product designed to benefit mankind, science devised weapons to destroy humanity. They could be deployed to every realm of the earth, land, sea, air, and even space. Highly sophisticated ballistic missiles were capable of vaporizing entire cities and their populaces. In the hands of rogue countries, they were a threat to life on Earth.

The scientific invention of weapons became an excruciating dilemma for the human race. Their deadly use in war was predictable, but their uncontrolled availability to the general public was devastating. With money, anyone could purchase weapons legally or illegally. As a result, the world became one huge overflowing arsenal. The personal use of guns brought death, carnage, and suffering to people of all walks of life. They were used to settle individual and family disputes, drive by road shootings assassinations, holdups, murders, racial discrimination, and target practice to improve man's ability to kill. The belief that people were entitled to own deadly weapons as protection against others that would do them harm was like the tail wagging the dog. Over time, civilian use of guns and the subsequent death rate rivaled the casualties from two world wars. With a gun in his hand, man had no fear; it inflated his manly ego and provided a false sense of invincibility. It was common practice to hunt wild animals for food that adhered to the rules of survival, but to destroy wildlife for the sake of inflating man's ego and then call it a sport was a disillusioned pastime for a human being.

The uncontrolled thinning out of wildlife to preserve habitat use for man would eventually backfire. He would become the hunted instead of the hunter. The foe that tracked man would loom on the horizon as his worst nightmare. His knees would wobble, his breath would come in gasps, and his legs would not support his weight. Only then would he know the fear and despair that his quarries felt facing death. With the indiscriminate destruction of the world's wildlife came the ultimate realization that man could not face the future alone. As the only remaining predator on Earth, his worst enemy was his own kind. It confirmed Darwin's theory that the weak shall perish and the strong shall inherit the earth.

The only beneficiaries who would survive man's destructive tendencies would be God and time. To improve man's standing on his planet, it was obvious that his inhuman treatment of his own species required restraint. Although his birthright assured him the rite of passage, it contained no license to kill, maim, torture, or enslave other members of the human race. Those who practiced these atrocities dehumanized God's special creation. As man evolved, his only hope of shedding these degrading tendencies was for those dehumanizing tendencies to wane and disappear. This would upgrade his image to allow his acquisition of the seven qualities that identified human beings. To suffer hereditary malfeasance would result in self debasement for the one creation God had selected for his greatest experiment. The human equation for the sanity of life permitted a double standard; man had no qualms about conceiving life and little concern about taking it.

When the people of the world considered that the phenomenal scientific achievements were advancing civilization, they could not discount their dedication. No faction on Earth could rival their commitment to improve mankind's welfare. The research and development of both pure and applied science furnished man with all the material comforts and luxuries to make his sojourn on Earth more enjoyable. Their marvels complemented every field of human endeavor, agriculture, manufacturing, medical, home, business, community, and even warfare. From the 1700s through the 1800s the methods of production changed slowly. After that they rose sharply with the industrial revolution. The budding chemical industry and new technologies drastically changed man's world with automation, computers, and a push-button society. The endless flow of improved technology and products transformed his home into a place of luxury and comfort. Unfortunately, concentrating on obtaining material possessions became an obsession that ruled most people's lives. In a developing world, this need was a natural ambition, but the craving for material things required restraint that people did not seem to possess.

One of the most perplexing values of some human beings was their indifference to the sanctity of life. The universal standard for human reproduction was that members of the opposite sex unite to perpetuate life. To ensure continuance of this process, God selected females as his surrogates to preserve the human dynasty on Earth. This sacred trust also contained a seed of morality and responsibility to its benefactor. Ignoring this binding covenant with the creator would jeopardize the spiritual bond between them.

The first sign of movement in the embryo signaled the beginning of life. No mortal had the moral right to abort life unless the mother's life was at stake. What God gave so freely could not be discarded so casually. Abortion was also a violation of Franklin D. Roosevelt's Four Freedoms petition of 1940, granting the right of life to every human being on Earth, all pregnancies must be carried to term and that adoption guarantees the sanctity of life. Nations that legislated for or against abortion were violating the mutual bond between a mother and her creator. Breaking it was only the mother's choice. Man did not consider the divine gift of life as miraculous.

Unfortunately, the eternal triangle of birth, life, death, and an afterlife was not immune to disruptions. His journey could be terminated at any moment by inappropriate or reckless actions. His somewhat perilous adventure though life was a recompense of the time continuum. God's embodiment contained in all of creation was an exclusive endowment for man. Enshrined in his physical being was the spiritual lineage that provided humans with a soul. With death, this inheritance becomes infinite and embraced by God for all eternity.

The eternal triangle was not man's to trifle with. It existed as the creator's formula for life on Earth. Humans were not the only life form exposed to the insensitivity of man. The indiscriminate practice of unauthorized poaching of the earth's wildlife was a violation of international law. Some nations turned a blind eye to the practice, allowing commercial interests to exploit and slaughter protected species for their body parts. Consequently, some species of birds, animals, and fish were destroyed to the point of extinction. Body parts were sold to the public for food, to cure ills, promote virility, and extend life expectancy. This resulted in passing down ancient myths and remedies by people who had no interest in preserving the chain of life on Earth, especially when these remedies and cures were readily available at corner pharmacies. Adding to this unlawful practice was the depletion of priceless metals, fossil fuels, and over-fishing the world's oceans. Exploiting and squandering the world's resources amounted to robbing its irreplaceable riches for profit.

With the rule of law in the world's criminal system, thieves usually received some sort of punishment for their crimes. In the case of man, he was facing a life sentence for raping his planet. Did he have the right to tamper with the evolutionary process? Every time a species of fauna became extinct because of man's actions, another life form that depended on it for sustenance was threatened. It was a vicious cycle, disrupting the progression of life on Earth. More importantly, it raised the question, "Who would fill the vacuum and replace the diversity of life on Earth?" a process that was 400 million years in the making. Man was incapable of creating life and was limited to reproducing his own species. It was a foregone conclusion that when he stood high on the hill to survey his domain, he would realize that alone he could not survive. The irresponsible disruption of the natural progression of life would eventually make him a prime candidate for the fossil record.

Not all of man's transgressions were of a destructive nature. In judging the global performance of the scientific establishment, civilization could not have been possible without their discoveries and unending dedication. One branch of science stood out above all others. The medical establishment achieved a balance of purpose in honoring God's mandates to preserve life. Their research and development introduced miraculous benefits for mankind, including stem cell research, genetic engineering, birth control, in vitro fertilization, extension of life expectancy, and many advances to maintain life and prevent human suffering. However, on several occasions scientific projects and religious doctrines had adverse effects on the planet's capacity to cope with overpopulation. Scientific extension of life expectancy, religion's intolerance of birth control, plus encouragement of human reproduction contributed to overpopulating the planet. This explosion of humanity over-exceeded the world's resources to grow and feed the masses. Consequently, ten to twenty thousand people died each year from hunger and famine.

At one end of the spectrum, man was committed to preserving life, but at the other end he was destroying it by overpopulating the planet. There was a bright side to human accomplishments that deserved eulogizing. Man's reign on Earth was not without moments of glory, especially when he received his credentials as God's superior being. There was an outstanding segment of Earth's population that rated celebrity status. They exemplified all the qualities and standards God had set during his attempt to create a perfect species—unselfish individuals, dedicated people whose voices, deeds, and actions made a difference to improving life on Earth. Devoid of self-serving acts and thoughts, they were devoted to serving God by respecting and extending tolerance to others. These qualities were at the top of the list to qualify one as a special being. They expected no earthly rewards, only a deep satisfaction of giving more to life than it gave them in return.

Man's over-concern about his human image fostered many crowning achievements to burnish his self esteem. He founded The American *Humane* Association in 1877 for the prevention of cruelty to children. The American Humane Society was established to prevent cruelty to animals. In 1940 the four freedoms stated that all human beings were born free and equal in dignity and universal rights. Many transgressions by humans were forbidden, including slavery, and cruel and degrading treatment and punishment..

A declaration in 1948 advocated basic social, economic, and civil rights for every human being. In spite of man's grandiose intentions, it became obvious that he required laws to restrain his uninhibited animal instincts. In man's mental progression and perilous journey to adopt life, it became clear that he could not do so alone. The burden of evolving from animal to human form was overwhelming. In reality he lived in a house of mirrors, and the only visible image was his own reflection. Had he looked deeper into the mirror of life, he would have seen his savior with outstretched arms offering hope, guidance, and eternal salvation.

To offset man's difficulty to build a responsible society on Earth, there were dedicated humanitarians. Founded in 1863, the Red Cross was devoted to relieve human suffering from natural disasters, war, and even during times of peace when there was a need. Their global reach extended to all of humanity regardless of race, nationality, or religion. The Salvation Army was also a worldwide Christian organization with a semi military structure. It provided food, shelter, and clothing to the needy. They administered to the forgotten part of society seeking spiritual salvation. These were the poor, needy, and downtrodden members of society. Both of these organizations exemplified the best in the human race. They were God's true and unrecognized apostles.

In trying to understand the human character—what could have possessed earthlings to step out of character and misuse God's gift of intelligence? In doing so, he put the future of his planet in jeopardy. Civilization had provided him with every luxury, comfort, and form of enjoyment, but not spiritual security. Material wealth was fleeting and unreliable in the long run. To find inner peace of mind, man needed reality checks on his thoughts and reasoning processes. Without divine guidance he required self analysis to assure that God's mandates were being fulfilled. Serenity, peace, and contentment were all available to mankind without a price tag. Only one power in the universe was capable of enriching man, and the rewards were free for the asking. The greatest investment he could make, one that paid the highest dividends, was faith in God. His outreach to humanity was unwavering and had spanned centuries in concert with time.

Since the dawn of history, mankind had never known complete peace and tranquility. Human beings had one humiliating and insurmountable flaw. They lacked one of the seven qualities that would glorify their race: no tolerance for other life forms on Earth, including their own species. Unending wars against humanity was a revival of primeval instincts and behavior. It stripped mankind of their ability to achieve perfection. At some place on Earth, hostilities or threat of war raged, tribe against tribe, warlord against warlord, family against family, religion against religion, and nations assaulting other nations. Wars were fought for power, wealth, territory acquisition, regional influence, and outright aggression. The specter of death and annihilation had always haunted man's thoughts. In retrospect, a similar condition occurred millions of years ago, when early life forms made their first pilgrimage from the sea onto land. All primitive life was confronted with a hostile and combative world. After millions of years, that condition remained unchanged, only man had moved its intensity to a new level of hostility. This new dimension of irresponsibility threatened the evolutionary process and did little to improve man's standing as a selected creation. The overdue attempts by man to moderate his excesses did not justify or excuse his inhumanity to humanity. The unraveling of history did not forgive the human race for past atrocious behavior and the horrifying casualties. They could encircle the earth twice around with a human chain of bodies laid side-by-side. The greedy, corrupt, and those prone to war could walk over the corpses without a backward glance or show of remorse. Without a conscience, this conduct was unmistakable proof that man had never shed his bestial instincts or lost his predatory ways.

With all its exalted capabilities, the human brain resembled a delicate scale. Excessive stress could tip its balance in one of two directions: good or bad, right or wrong. Man was often bewildered by his higher intelligence. He could not reconcile his mind's evolutionary transformation to the rite of passage. This transparency of character was never more evident than when his intelligence was being tested. In some ways, human beings were inflicted with an inferiority complex and were constantly attempting to reinvent themselves. Not content with the natural order of life, man resorted to creating artificial life and cloning animals with an eye on cloning humans in the future—perhaps to surpass God's creativity. Replicating life by mortals violated the evolutionary process, and reducing man to robotic form was not only dehumanizing, it was impossible without an alliance with time.

This uncomplimentary case against man is one of unbelievable irresponsibility.

In his challenge to become of age, he was being tested by the creator in every phase of his development. The finer attributes of mankind were honed and refined for more than one million years by time's effect on the evolutionary process. His unannounced arrival on Earth was a pivotal contribution to creation and life on the planet. Human beings were the only species selected, pampered, and groomed to perform a specific mission in life: to love, honor, and acknowledge the creator. No other life form had ever been chosen to rise through the evolutionary ranks and reach this level of intelligence. His only handicap, without divine oversight, was to use his intelligence wisely. This slight to man was not accidental but deliberate to expedite his rite of passage, a feat he must accomplish on his own.

In spite of his superior mental abilities, man never reached the high degree of perfection God had envisioned. In his rise to global stardom, he was still serving his apprenticeship, a work in progress. Without conformation of his roots, man was a lost spirit, orphaned, unclaimed, and handicapped at birth with questionable parentage. In spite of these difficulties, he managed to build a thriving civilization.

In the overall process there was one dominate liability that overshadowed all other aspects of man's daily life: he adopted a monetary system that bred greed and corruption and downgraded human values. For a majority of the masses it was a no-win situation. They were chained to a revolving treadmill, and its momentum was so rapid they could not keep pace with life in general. His species was tottering on the brink of a dismal and uncertain future. There was no turning back. God and time would not grant humans a second chance.

With all the challenges and distractions in man's life, was there a reward for living a well-balanced life, with God at its center? For all of humanity who yearned for peace and salvation, there was an echo to the silence of eternity. Its clarity could be defined as infinite contentment and security in God's embrace. His covenant with time assured that he was the power and the glory forever more. For those lost people who were torn between non-belief and a faith in God, there was a solution. Human beings have no way of personally communicating with God, except by prayer. Those who seek help and salvation become recipients of the most awesome and rewarding experience felt by mankind. They are deeply humbled if God responds to their prayers. It reassures them that they are not alone to combat the difficulties in life. Because of God's benevolent gesture, should man expect deliverance for making unwise decisions that violate his mandates and exercise poor judgment? The creator could not be held accountable for the inept working of the human mind, which was man's responsibility by his birthright. It was one thing to be appreciative of his good will, but it had to be earned and not taken for granted.

Over time it became clear that humans had not created a perfect world and was always in constant turmoil from unending wars. In 1920 an international organization called the League of Nations was created for the purpose of maintaining peace. It never succeeded because nations refused to cooperate, and the organization was later dissolved. As countries' appetite for war continued, a new organization was founded in 1945, called the United Nations. The UN became a global forum, with a mandate to ensure peace and security on a worldwide scale. It advocated nuclear disarmament and the end of testing weapons of mass destruction. Unfortunately the UN lacked the will, monetary resources, and military manpower to enforce their mandate. Without them, they were incapable of policing the world. Eventually they became known as peacekeepers after a conflict ended and a platform to debate global issues was founded. The UN proved to be ineffective in preserving world order.

Not all scientists and theologians were at odds in agreeing on the source of creation. Many open-minded converts of each faction found a relationship between God and science. In 1939 the science world's Big Bang theory, describing the birth of the universe, had a positive effect on the Catholic Church. They officially pronounced that the theory was in accordance with the bible. This vindication of scientific findings was a major breakthrough in resolving the great controversy. Unfortunately it was not universally acknowledged by other major religions. In the ongoing debate to establish credibility to their views, both parties were at a disadvantage because of their inability to recognize that the creator's embodiment was enshrined in all of creation. How could any mortal live in their magnificent surroundings and not feel Gods presence? Even the blind could sense and bond with the creator. In their unending world of darkness, he was their only light to provide companionship and security, offering comfort in the knowledge that they were not alone.

Deciphering and labeling of scientific discoveries focused on the past and present evolution of the physical universe. The more revelations they uncovered, the more religion's claim of divine creation was strengthened. The one problem scientists could not resolve was that their discoveries were often misleading or inaccurate. When the unfavorable verbal criticism finally died down, most of their achievements proved accurate. The same denigration was applied to religion, but it could not shake a faith that had endured for more than two thousand years. In keeping with the scientific dogma that seeing is believing, cosmologists observed and theorized to explain the workings of the universe. Their findings were based on the science of physics and visual sight by astrologers. One of the foremost debatable questions puzzling scientists was the possibility that dark matter existed. Was this the energy force that expands and drives the universe? In past years scientists offered many theories to explain an evolving universe—a parallel universe, perhaps a collapsed or collided bubble, or a two-dimensional universe, to name a few—all consistent within scientific parameters but inconclusive. It became evident that man could not build sandcastles on thin air.

Scientific efforts to understand the working universe will always be unattainable, until they redefine their definition of time. The potency of the time continuum is equivalent to that of dark energy, if it exits. Before we take the spotlight off science, what is their prediction for the future of the universe? Based on normal conditions for an evolving universe, with no distractions from unknown sources, they suggest two theories: one of a stable universe, and another of an unstable universe. When we consider the past twenty billion years of creative history, it is logical to assume that everything God created had a limited existence. There was no question the universe was unstable when witnessing the life and death of heavenly bodies throughout the firmament. The fact that space is curved suggests that an ever-expanding universe will eventually complete a circular path, return to its original starting point, collide, or collapse. It is also possible that the universe will expand outward like a giant rubber band and reach the extent of its elasticity, snap back, and collapse. In either event, if this occurs, the Big Bang similarity (the birth of the universe) and the Big Crunch similarity (the end of the universe) will come true. Ironically, the late *eminent* scientist Albert Einstein's theory of relativity implied that the universe had a beginning and ending. Eventually, if the universe implodes or collides the remnant matter will condense into a hyper-dense state. This mass will become the nucleus for a new genesis, and the process of creation will continue through infinity.

For individuals who seek an answer to the age-old question *does God exist*, the answer is actually a matter of faith, and they must walk a fine line between illusion and reality. In the final analysis, it is personal awareness of his surroundings that determines the answer. Only here will the human sensory organs perceive God's embodiment enshrined in all of creation. The eyes, nose, ears, taste buds, and special nerve endings on both hands were designed explicitly for this purpose. When man stood on the threshold of life, he only had to step over to find God. With faith it would immediately envelop him with a protective blanket of sublime love and devotion. That unbridled affection would surpass all of life's worldly attachments. Acknowledging his creator would be man's most rewarding and defining moment. In return it imparts a desire for recognition. By accepting God, man will achieve his manifest destiny and a passport for eternal life.

Seeing: God's presence was visible to the naked eye in the aura of light that permeates the universe, a divine illumination that resonates even in the darkness of night. The splendor and beauty that man observes in his surroundings are an indication of his presence. When we observe the breathtaking tranquility of the firmament, are we not enraptured with God's accomplishments? Does it not awaken a close relationship that complements our mortality? Those who welcome an early morning sunrise see the awakening of God's essence in all of nature. The spellbinding aura of light soothes the mind, bringing peace and contentment. When a mother first gazes into the eyes of her newborn, does she not feel equality with her creator? Does the immaculate silver sheen that decorates our oceans and beaches not impart serenity and peace and awareness of God's presence? When lovers embrace in tender affection, do they not feel God's approval and devotion to their union? The intricate works of artists, craftsmen, and musicians—do they not embrace and emulate God's love of creation? Even the falling rain conveys God's tears for the soul of man.

Hearing: Because God's spiritual embodiment is in all of creation, do we not hear his voice resonate in the sounds of nature? We are enraptured by the sopranos, baritones, altos, and tenors of the bird world. Do not these melodious sounds resound with God's message of tranquility and contentment? Do we not hear God's voice from those who preach his doctrines?

Smell: When we inhale the elixirs of our food and the fragrance of our surroundings, do they not stimulate the vibrancy of those scents God breathes into his creations?

Taste: When we consume food that God provided, do we not acknowledge his commitment by giving thanks? We take a moment to express our appreciation for the centuries of culturing and nurturing by the creator for man's benefit.

Touch: During our lifetime, are we not privileged to touch many of God's creations?

This defining moment of mutual contact is one of awakening. It imparts God's spiritualism to the one who touches. The intimacy of the sensation lingers as a constant reminder of his presence and devotion to mankind.

As time left its imprint on man's consciousness, the hostilities between religion and science abated somewhat in the middle of the twentieth century. They reached a stalemate because neither profession could come to grips with resolving their differences. Both factions had become conscious of their excesses and capacity for evil. At times their arguments simmered just below the surface and then burst into flames, causing further doubt and confusion. The ongoing dispute invaded the privacy of man's sensibilities, depriving him the satisfaction of knowing his roots. The prolonged debate was never-ending, and neither faction could find a common ground to resolve their differences.

The impasse was an unacceptable deterrent because man needed a stable foundation to base his life and future on. The simmering controversy raised the question: which party was better qualified to resolve the debate? The scientific establishment had labored for more than four hundred years to prove their case. The religious community had persevered for two thousand years to bolster their beliefs. The contest was decidedly one-sided in favor of science. It was a matter of making an analysis of physical evidence against the written word of man.

However, based strictly on physical evidence, conclusions can be misleading. Scientific documentation was gathered after the fact. They confirmed creation took place but offered no explanation of why or who was responsible for the miracle. Religion had no such doubts that the holy scriptures explained the source of creation. Yet their theologians should have considered that with physical proof and a direct line of communication with the creator, man would have no need for religion. Comparing the two most powerful forces on Earth, religion was responsible for guiding mankind through the adversities of life. Religious indoctrination was formulated to fill the mental disconnect between man and his creator to instill a genuine moral and spiritual contribution to ensure man a life of contentment. Man's attempts to accept credibility and a belief in the holy scriptures was elemental to his existence. Instilling core spiritual values, devoid of divine influence, would be a daunting challenge. The success or failure of people to bond with their creator was dependent on time. Realizing that the arguments about creation were often an exercise in futility, was it reasonable to expect a degree of civility? Their narrow avenue of discourse focused on a divine source or the natural happenings of science. At intervals their withering arguments bordered on hypocrisy.

A fitting example is of religious officials who ridiculed the validity of scientific accomplishments, particularly in establishing a defiant and unrelenting position. They diminished their professional standing. Whereas they had no valid physical proof to confirm divine creation, they discounted scientific discoveries that confirmed the relationship between God and time. It took astronomers, paleontologists, and geologists just two hundred years to piece together the physical record of creation, a monumental achievement considering it took twenty billion years to accumulate. Downgrading the efforts of one profession to make points for their own incapability diminishes their credibility as a competent voice for the truth.

The possibility of a spiritual relationship between God and man was at times unintelligible. Over time, could man fulfill his destiny to find peace with God?

God could not be seen, yet his embellishment is spellbinding when visualized in the profusion of nature. God cannot be touched, yet he imparts spiritualism to sooth and comfort the heart of man. God could not be heard, yet his message is immortalized in the scriptures which govern the conscience of mankind. His sacred mandates invades the privacy of all, but is offensive to none, for it projects eternal love and compassion for his chosen people.

One of the disadvantages of being human was coping with the constant mental stress. Buried at the core of this distress was the nagging verification of his birthright. The main obstacle to this confirmation was the great controversy: why was it so important to confirm one's roots? Mainly because the past is what determines the future. Man was under the false impression that his planet was indestructible and immune to the predetermined lifecycle imposed on all of creation. The vast majority of people on Earth had little concern about creation or their origins. Why muddy the water if the answer had no profound effect on their lives? The irony is that humans can ignore hereditary confirmation for only so long before it leaves them blindsided by time. Before his time ran out, it was necessary that he knew who he was, where he came from, and what his purpose in life was. In recent years scientific discoveries and theories have vastly improved the world's understanding of how the universe works. However, they remain in the dark as to who was responsible for the miraculous birthing act. Their stated beliefs and convictions of both factions needed to be compared and brought into perspective.

What source or element of science was capable of achieving the following:

- Controlling and formulating the evolutionary process?
- Providing meaning and purpose to creation?
- Altering the normal creation process and introduce select life forms?
- Determining how the universe thrives and expands?

What miracle did science evoke to elevate man to prominence as the most intelligent life form on Earth? What designer in science can take credit for creating our planet and its phenomenal beauty?

Scientists' tenuous efforts to label the source of creation was ongoing but an improbable undertaking. To their credit, a dedicated research faction was successful in deciphering the human genetic code by using DNA to confirm ancestral lineage. Gene-sequestering technology brought primitive geology into modern perspective. Tracing man's ascension through the ages was progress, but one has to remember that genetic coding occurred long before the birth of man. It originated during the genesis when the creator committed his embodiment into all matter. God's commitment to the genesis was the basis genetic containment of all creation.

It is reasonable to believe that science will not find the answer to universal creation under a microscope. It is beyond their expertise. God's DNA inclusion preempted human's and embodies the living soul of man. The four hundred years that scientists devoted to theorizing on universal creation was an unproductive effort, here today; gone tomorrow. Cosmology—the study of the universe—had been constant but subject to change with every advanced theory. In spite of all their successes, scientists worked in a vacuum without a complete understanding of how the universe works.

They describe it as a formation of two basic theories: the theory of relativity and quantum mechanics. Explaining them is irrelevant because these two theories are known to be inconsistent and incompatible with each other and therefore not valid. Recognizing this inconsistency, scientists are constantly seeking a new theory known as the Grand Unified Theory. That goal will never become a reality until they define time as a medium and not just a passing interval between two events. The space time continuum exists as a mechanism that thrives and expands the universe because God willed it so.

There is a common denominator that could resolve the great controversy. Mankind's impression of time is illusional, impersonal, and fleeting. It dates back to the introduction of language and writing. The public treat it with indifference and only monitor its coming and going as a formality of life. There is a disconcerting problem with this reasoning. Any power that has the capacity to enforce transitional change should not be considered a non entity. Science and religion needed to reassess their interpretations of the time continuum. Until they do, the debate over creation will remain a moot issue. The dictionary defines time as "a measured or measurable period during which an action, process, or condition exists or continues." This explanation is superficial and inconclusive. It does not explain the phenomenal physical transformations that appear in its wake. Time is a medium, a conduit with the capacity to carry out God's will, and it's responsible for creation, evolution, and the expanding universe.

In applying the dictionary's definition of birth and death, the interim period of life becomes sterile and meaningless. As with all life forms, humans are born, reproduce, grow old, and die. They do so not by the passing of time but because the medium is the regulatory conduit for the lifecycle. The incredible changes that occur are unmistakable proof of its volatility. It is reasonable to ask the question, "Does the passage of time create change, or is the medium the purveyor of God's grand design?" Abrupt physical changes do not occur instantly or at random but only over long periods of time. As a perpetual component of creation, time is incapable of starting or stopping. Like the creator it has no beginning or ending. It is an infinite abstract, theoretical, impersonal, and has no pictorial representation. When we recognize God, we must also accept time as his counterpart, for they are inseparable. Humans accept time as a point of reference, an accommodation, like the air they breathe. The infinite power of time was never acknowledged by science or religion. Failure to recognize that God and time were cosponsors of creation would be man's greatest blunder. They were the only safety net standing between him and eternity.

Without time's infinite force, the evolution of man and Earth would cease and become dormant. The significance of the relationship between God and time is truly the most revealing and profound revelation ever experienced by mankind. Their creative energies are exactly the same in every detail except one. Only God can furnish meaning and purpose to the creation process. Because of the similarities between the two, there is no one event in the history of creation accredited to God that cannot be attributed to time. They act in concert and are inseparable. The comparison suggests that man is long overdue to accept that God and time are one and the same, the one unified force responsible for creation that science cannot label. Acceptance of this revelation would close the offensive gap between religion and science, resolve the great controversy, and bring a new perspective to the creation process.

When we apply the impact of time to the human lifecycle, there is a morbid ring to the event of death. Yet, if God's creations did not have a terminal ending, evolution would not work. The renewal of life on our planet would become redundant. Earth would exist as a colossal empty graveyard, without proof that humans ever existed because they would have inevitably become instinct. This was one consolation for man: knowing life had an ending increased his efforts to achieve a bond with God before his time ran out.

Although humans acknowledged time as a matter of fact, they were also enamored with its inflexibility and invented instruments—ones that record its coming and going in seconds, minutes, hours, days, weeks months, years, and centuries—to monitor and record its passing. Man's respect for its aging effects was crucial to his existence. Time was his best friend until middle age, when it could then become his worst enemy. As a requisite necessary for life, man had to accept that time was on God's side and not man's. Man had to regulate his life to accommodate its passing—a time to be born, live, wake up, go to work and return, get married, have children, and then face death and culminate his bond with the creator.

One of the most dramatic examples of God and time's creativity was repetitive universe building. Its physical chronology is a duplicate of the life and death cycles applied to all of creation. To properly examine the pre-birth of the universe, it is necessary to analyze the age of darkness. This hallowed and endless void was hosted by only two entities, God and time. They existed as a catalytic life force that emancipated the age of darkness, extending light to its extremities. However extensive this period, time's pendulum was in motion long before the physical universe was born. This period in theology was considered a day of rest. In reality, the dark age was not a benign or unproductive era; it required an entity to inspire ingenuity and endless preparation to make creation a reality. These requirements only originated with the creator and not the science of chemistry. Because instantaneous creation is not possible, transforming a dark void into one with light required endless amounts of time, and this medium only responded to the will of God. To substantiate time's indelible imprint on the universe, one only has to observe the overhead firmament. It was home to the procession of creation, stretching across the vast cosmos and hiding in the archives of Earth. Time was an essential ingredient to all natural events, the life cycle, global phenomenon, changes in seasons and tides, and the movement of celestial bodies along with the evolutionary chain of life on Earth.

Although humans acknowledged time only as a part of living, they became enamored with its inflexibleness and invented instruments to monitor and record its passing. Calendars provided a graphic record of past and future events. As a universal powerhouse for change, nothing was immune to its relentless pressure. Man realized that his life was arbitrarily, that it could end at birth or endure to reach a ripe old age. With persistence it became a race against time. Man's respect for its potency was critical to his existence. In his early life it was his best friend, and after middle age it could become his worst enemy. As people age, they must accept that time is on God's side and not man's. As a recipient of the medium's intolerance, people had to regulate their lives to its passing. A time to be born, live, to wake up, go to work, and return, get married, have children, face death, and culminate his bond with his creator.

With all of its complexities, the physical universe functioned as a time-powered clock, recording its passing not in small intervals but in centuries and ages, in the process accomplishing two objectives. Comparing God's immunity to the passing of time was in sharp contrast to man's allotted lifecycle. With the passing of time, man had little to show for a fruitful life, unless he married, had children, and found a mutual bond with his creator. Because life is considered short by human standards, it was never fully appreciated by man.

He took his turn at living but never considered that it would take one million years for his species to evolve. He constantly complained about his life in general, depression, insecurity, an unhappy marriage, disrespectful children, government, taxes, and having to labor most of his life. To compensate for these debilitating events, he was constantly attempting to reinvent himself. Unfortunately, it was an unattainable goal, for time was not on his side.

When questioning time's function in relation to creation, humans should have considered the consequences if it stopped or became inactive, especially if they accepted the dictionary's interpretation of a measured period between two events. Without this medium there would be no driving force to expand and perpetuate the universe. All life would hang in suspended animation. God would be rendered impotent, unable to create. Chemistry could not be active, leaving science without a sponsor, and the evolutionary process would grind to a halt. In the final analogy there would be no passing interval between two events. Can these devastating events be attributed to a benign period? The answer should be obvious.

In man's efforts to circumvent time, he considered his life short and constantly looked for ways to extend it. The topic of reincarnation always intrigued people looking for immortality. Reincarnation rekindled an old adage, "Everybody wants to go to heaven, but nobody wants to die." Some individuals firmly believe in an afterlife. Others scoff at reincarnation. The renewal of life was believed to be an after-death experience, where the spirit of the deceased reappears on Earth in another form. This is not considered a physical transition but a rebirth of one's spirit. For mortals, preserving one's spirituality was entrusted solely to God, and its final resting place is in God's keeping. Man's pursuit of a meaningful life eventually changed when he realized spiritualism was more essential to a bountiful life than materialism. This revelation—when he took refuge in the holy bible—was one of the most profound moments in his life. It was one of man's greatest achievements and a tribute to the fertility of the human mind. It supplemented the absence of divine influence over man's mental process. The bible's message provided a moral and spiritual roadmap for man to live by. It was the most sacred and revered formula ever written and was considered the word of God. The message transcended time and resonated worldwide to become the guideline for human behavior. The mandates eventually became a conscience for mankind, insulating him from the insecurities that came with life. The contents of the bible included seventy-three books for Catholics and some Protestants, sixty-six for other Protestants, and thirty-nine for Jews. These sacred doctrines provided a single purpose for man in essays, stories, poetry, and laws. Although revised one hundred ninety-five times, the King James version first appeared in 1611.The spiritual contents not only furnished meaning and purpose to man's life, they also tested his courage, resolve, and convictions. When man fully accepted its mandates and embraced God, he would achieve his manifest destiny.

The beginnings of contemporary religion were founded based on the teachings and beliefs of ancient priests and prophets. They lived and were exposed to events that occurred thousands of years ago. The holy scriptures had withstood the test of time until scientific discoveries of the physical universe questioned two paragraphs and their contents. As scientists delved into the birthing of heaven and Earth, they found strewn across the vastness of space the unmistakable remnants of God's past creations. By scientific dating methods, these cosmic fossils revealed dramatic findings. They confirmed that past generations of heavenly bodies produced astronomical periods of time. These revelations shook the religious establishment to its foundations. They did not coincide with biblical accounts of creation.

The worldwide quest to confirm the source of man's beginnings came to a head in 1871.This was the year Charles R. Darwin published his controversial book *The Origin of Species*, followed years later by *The Descent of Man*. The two books immediately provoked a storm of protest from theologians and disbelief in the public sector. His theories did not coincide with biblical accounts of creation. The concept that man evolved from apes rather than divine conception was unthinkable. It made Darwin's theories suspect in the religious community. Even mention of the word evolution initiated a scathing reply and became the most vilified work in the English language. "Darwinism" advocated that all life is related, that species evolve over time in response to natural selection and are replaced with new life forms. It explained that this was simply the way biology works and was the basic structuring of life on Earth. Factions of the religious community waged a relentless campaign to discredit Darwin's theories. Many repeated attempts were made to replace evolutionary concepts with biblical versions of creation in classrooms. These discordant parties had a tendency to distort reality to make their positions more palatable for public consumption. Even with the latest advances in genetics, physics, and biochemistry, his theories have withstood scientific scrutiny for more than a century and a half. As they age, they still accommodated the most advanced studies of science. One example of the dissidents' theories was called "intelligent design." It implied that some life forms appeared abruptly with their distinctive features already intact. This completely ignored the fact that instantaneous creation is not possible. The evolution of life is wholly dependent on time for gradual transitional change. Their intelligent design theory revived an old adage, "Which came first, the chicken or the egg?" Neither appeared abruptly. Those life forms with egg-laying capabilities evolved over long periods of time.

Over time the impact of Darwinism went through its own evolutionary transformation. People, educators, scientists, and some religious factions accepted his theories as valid. Yet the biblical version of creation still complicated man's legitimacy. Questionable origins, plus the fact that selected creation had never been implemented before, added to his confusion. The anatomical transformation of animal species into human form was the most spectacular innovation in the history of creation. The idea that God had committed his spiritual embodiment to the genesis changed man's concepts of the creative process. Because all matter contained God's divine essence, every creature shared a common kinship. There was no shame or hereditary dishonor to acknowledging animal ancestry, and before man's legendary arrival on Earth, members of the wildlife kingdom were the foremost intelligent life forms to inhabit the planet. Because of its superior intelligence and upright stature, the primate order was selected by God as the prototype of the human species. The fact that divine spirituality was incorporated into all matter should have united and not divided religion and science. Both could accept the biblical description of creation as a truism. Creating man and woman from Earth's matter raised another possibility. The earth's matter already contained the creator's DNA, which confirmed man was born of God.

When one considers the Bible's contents, we must remember that it was conceived more than two thousand years ago. It was written long before the birth of science. In fact, the word science was not even in man's vocabulary. The ancients lived in a world that did not revolve around the sun, only the holy land. After two decades the time lapse illustrates the frailty of human perception. The moral standards and spiritual integrity of the Bible were never in question, except for the two opening paragraphs in the book of Moses, called Genesis, where it was stated that God created heaven and Earth in six days and took one day to rest. The second paragraph describes the creation of man and woman from the dust of the ground. In six days God created light, separated day from night, made the heavens, water, land, plants, trees, fish, birds, animals, and man and woman. Setting aside what science and the public consider factual, these two paragraphs test our credibility. They cast doubts on the knowledge and mental capabilities of its authors. Throughout civilized history, no other document has made the spiritual impact and call for self analysis. It will always serve as the conscience for mankind. When originally written, the world was in turmoil, with unending wars and the enslavement of segments of humanity. The masses' only hope of ending their misery was spiritual salvation. History has shown that at times of crisis, someone always appears to save the day. In these difficult times, God's only son was granted life on Earth to save humanity. He offered the masses hope, peace, and salvation by acknowledging his father's divinity. This mutual covenant was the foremost reason God chose the human race as his selected creation. They had the unsurpassed wisdom to bring life and God's mandates into perspective.

In the early controversial years, the opening paragraph of Genesis was contested loudly and consistently by scientific factions. Over time the intensity faded into a minor discourse and became irrelevant. Nonbelievers and uninterested parties gave little thought too who or what was responsible for creation. Although man's written word could fade in time, its message lingered deep in people's unconscious, seeking confirmation. Theologians were content to let the debate fade and become a non issue. In the interest of validating mankind's lineage, paleontologists and anthropologist spent years searching and uncovering fossil evidence to confirm human evolution. In today's advanced society, should scriptures written centuries ago still be honored and revered? Factually, they were the only stable foundation supporting civilization in its present state. Without their guiding influence, man would have been unable to mold himself into the refined creation God envisioned. The binding message in the holy Bible had not changed over two centuries, only the actions and behavior of those who read its contents. Throughout history, no other holy document had made the spiritual impact and call for self analysis. When originally written, the world was in turmoil with unending wars and the enslavement of segments of humanity. The masses' only hope of ending their misery was spiritual salvation. When God granted his son earthly form and a mission on Earth to save humanity from itself, he had faith in the authenticity of his selected people. It resulted in betrayal and his son enduring the supreme sacrifice for our sins.

In the contemporary world, God's words brought a semblance of human values and civility to the masses. The need for spiritual enlightenment persists as strongly today as in centuries past. Interpretations of ancient scriptures and verbally preaching their message to the public in a modern dialogue and perspective required considerable skills. The constant sermonizing of scriptures that embrace the past sometimes becomes redundant, if the message does not associate with the present. The Bible, like all of creation, is subjected to the pressure of time. If valid scientific evidence is discovered that conflicts with ancient scriptures, this should also be subjected to revision. For a document revised one hundred ninety-five times, one more will not diminish it spiritual value. A suggested starting point would be perpetual universe proliferation, with each one separated by an age of darkness, a striking resemblance to the biblical wording of *six days for creation, followed by a day of rest.*

Today when people view the overhead magnitude of star systems and entire galaxies, it taxes the mind to believe that the universe was created in six days, especially when considering it is currently still evolving into a super universe. Ancient religious scholars were incapable of determining the gestation period necessary for birthing an infant universe. Even in modern times, creationists insist that the earth is only ten thousand years old. They completely ignore the geological evidence of intermittent ice ages, earth stratification, and the fossil record of Earth. In pressing their case, they in fact question God's divinity and his covenant with time, which made creation possible. After four hundred years of sparring and controversy, it was obvious that mankind was long overdue to awaken from a lethargic dependence on the failure of religion and science, to set their houses in order. If the human species was to survive, it was mandatory for man to have a clear picture of his past to stake his future on. As a matter of professional courtesy, scientists' efforts to discredit the two paragraphs in the scriptures was grossly insensitive. Not only did it keep man uniformed of his origins, it lowered their professional standing. They questioned their own convictions concerning evolution. The transition over time began as a low degree of mentality and led to a higher level of intelligence. It mimics current beliefs that a child must learn to crawl before learning to walk.

In early times, scholars who authored the Bible had no knowledge or profound interest in universal creation. Obviously those early prognosticators had not achieved the learning curve of today's scientists or theologians. Taking this into consideration, do two minor infractions written in the Bible warrant four hundred years of friction between the world's most intelligent professions? Both border on hypocrisy. Even after two thousand years neither has identified the actual nature and function of time. They deserve to be censored for the severity of damage inflicted on mankind's sensibilities. Why were some professionals so intolerant of accepting concrete physical evidence that "speaks for itself"? It was self demeaning for both parties to distort or publish biased articles to promote their positions on creation.

One of the most outstanding achievements by scientists was deciphering the genetic code of human DNA. Gene sequestering traced man's origins back to his beginnings. Compared with the fossil record, it confirmed that the African primate's homeland was also the birthplace of mankind. The discovery was an absolute vindication of Darwinism. Religious factions can ill afford to turn a blind eye and ignore scientific discoveries that contest their beliefs. The relentless pendulum of time does not tolerate indifference. Religion needed to update and incorporate these discoveries into their sermons to encourage spiritual enlightenment. Without review and revision, their mission and credibility were at stake.

Looking into the future, it is only a matter of time before scientists discover extraterrestrial life in the universe. This inevitable revelation will be the second greatest event in the history of mankind, second only to creation itself. Life on Earth will never be the same. Our world will shrink in size and importance and so will its faith in religion. The fabric of man's life will unravel as his fascination is diverted to exploring the far horizons of space, an enticing challenge. To By severing his earthly constraints, he would become a universal voyager, possibly to become a member of a federation of planets. To be accepted, humans would have a monumental obstacle to overcome, such as having to justify a history of war, death, and destruction toward their own species, a dark legacy that could contaminate the thoughts of more advanced civilizations.

The greatest casualty in discovering extraterrestrial life would be religion, as the holy scriptures do not mention life beyond our earthly borders. Sacred doctrines would be consigned to the archive of infinity, relics of the past. Religious institutions would flounder and fall out of favor. How humiliating for humans to learn that they are not the only superior intelligence in the universe. Time is the greatest threat to religion's survival. If they do take concrete steps to prepare their followers for the future by setting their house in order, they will lose their jurisdiction as the world's guiding light. Spiritual leaders would be forced to face reality. Time is an evolutionary power that enforces change. The medium is never idle or on the side of mortals and is only God's to command. When we regress in time and contemplate the rise of civilization and its core religious base, it is only made possible by a complement of dedicated people seeking salvation. Their center of operations was the natural world God had prepared for them.

Man's artificial paradise of plastic, concrete, and glass were also necessary to advance civilization but did little to satisfy man's spiritual needs. Sadly, the universal acceptance of God was not possible. After one million years of evolutionary refinement, what possessed some individuals who received God's gift of life to deny its benefactor? There existed in the human race people known as atheists. They mingled among the populace, self contained and devoid of any need for a divine attachment. Man was not a whole person without a spiritual bond with the creator. His understanding of life was an empty and insecure journey, always fearful of when the next hammer would fall to test his staying power. He was not anointed by God to be self serving, to live in a spiritual vacuum, devoid of any meaning or purpose. To acknowledge God was man's purpose in life. Without this relationship they became the miscarriages of creation. Life did not guarantee a free pass with no strings attached. Lacking a disciplined spiritual incentive, atheists' lives were wasted. To circumvent time, they needed self analysis and to take an account of their lives. They needed to answer one crucial question: where will I spend eternity? The answer was a foregone conclusion—exiled to the darkness and obscurity of eternity without recourse. Indifferent about his gift of life, the atheist offered nothing in return. These misfits who denied God were without conscience, their disbeliefs rarely outspoken but disguised to prevent recognition, knowing they were not the mainstream of Earth's humanity.

Another misconception of many people was their view of life after death. Some devout religious believers predicted that living a life of sin and denying God was punishable by banishment to purgatory, in the fiery bowels of Earth. Yet hell was not of God's making. By denying God, man created his own living hell on earth. The creator's enrichment of spirit was embodied in all of creation, and for man it represented his eternal soul. Upon death it was reunited with his creator for all eternity.

In the progressive movement of religion to establish prominence on Earth, it is important to take note of a pure but primitive type of religion practiced by native cultures called animism, which is the belief that their creator's spiritual embodiment exists in all of nature, including animals. Here in the natural world they found an intimacy with his embodiment and made no attempts to change it. Primitive cultures embraced nature because it was the key to their survival. By this close association, the creator's presence could not be avoided. Lest we forget, man's perceptive features were designed primarily for this purpose. This unrivaled demonstration of spiritual equality between man and his creator was never duplicated by contemporary religion. How is it that primitive, uncivilized people with immature mentality could recognize the creator's spiritual presence in all things when today, people with fully developed intellect could not? It was unfortunate that animism was not adopted into modern theology; it would have defused the belief that God is invisible.

The persuasive power of religion eventually became the most powerful force on Earth. Its extended reach was global, with a spiritual attraction that surpassed any other worldly consideration. Over time eleven major religions rose to prominence on Earth: Christianity, Judaism, Islam, Hinduism, Buddhism, Jainism, Confucianism, Taoism, Shintoism, Sikhism, and Zoroastrianism. All were based on a belief of a supreme deity, a prophet, or holy doctrines. Because there was no verbal or direct communications between man and God, religions were conceived to fill the gap in man's untutored mental disconnect with his creator. The birth of man was not an act of gratitude but one of necessity. God required recognition for billions of years of his perfecting creation. Religion's rise gave voice to those desires. By accepting the burden of man's future, they assumed an awesome responsibility. Their holy doctrines became man's lifeline to exist. Underlying their holy mission was the stigma of his birthright. Hidden among man's imperfections were the traits and instincts of his animal predecessors. When they surfaced, their tendencies were received as part of man's natural character or as an evil induced by a burdensome civilization. Lingering in the recesses of people's unconscious, these handicaps were considered an unexplained enigma. Unfortunately, the hierarchy of some religions were also infested with this hereditary malady. For a profession entrusted with spiritual perfection, their actions would test God's faith in man.

Many years after religion became institutionalized, they adopted commercial tendencies that conveyed the message that wealth was a necessity for spiritual gain. When assessing the rise of religion, it is apparent that all faiths do not share the same objective in preserving and respecting the sanctity of life. Some were more aggressive than others in spreading their power and influence around the world. In many instances their actions caused deadly results.

Their unholy adventures left a bloody imprint on history. One example was the Spanish conquest of South American natives in 1521. Initiated by the Spanish monarchy and the Catholic Church, their invading army butchered the people and pillaged the region in an attempt to obtain the gold and convert the "heathens" to Christianity. Throughout history, religious influence was responsible for numerous deadly conflicts on our planet. Their barbaric campaigns and religious intolerance was only subterfuge for spreading church influence into the new world. The Spanish army not only introduced metal armor and weapons but contagious diseases, which the native population had no immunity to, including measles, smallpox, and typhus. As a result, ninety-nine million people perished in the conflict and spread of disease. It was one of the first holocausts. Such was the lust for power and wealth in some religious hierarchies.

Another example of religious intolerance occurred in AD 1100, when European nobles conspired with the Catholic Church to send several large military expeditions to wage war on people of the Islamic faith. They recruited crusaders from Christian nations in Western Europe as holy knights. The invaders ravaged the Muslim region for two hundred years with one objective: to regain control of the holy land. The conflict eventually ended with a fragile truce. What moral authority does any religion hope to embrace when they violate God's holy sacraments and advocate destroying humanity? When they condone spilling man's blood, it contains God's blood, and our blood is his blood.

Another example of religion's strife was the thirty-year war of 1618. This was a civil conflict between Catholics and Protestants in Germany. More than three hundred years later the same religious faiths repeated their intolerance with bloodshed in Northern Ireland. These confrontations had a way of repeating themselves.

As an advocate for spiritual purity of the world's second largest religion, the Catholic Church suffered a bruising malignancy in 2009. It was beyond belief that a faith could not ensure the saintliness of their clergy. The church ordained pedophiles who hid their sexual orientation beneath clerical robes. These predators preyed on children in their parishes for more than fifty years before exposure. This frightful situation was not confined to the church. It occurred in youth organizations, schools, and families. One out of every three girls and one out of every five boys experienced sexual abuse before the age of eighteen. Adding to this situation, sick and sexually driven rapists were active in every culture. In spite of church embarrassment and hefty lawsuits in Catholic parishes, it was not clear whether the Vatican took steps to eradicate the problem.

Even with depraved offenses against God and humanity, people yearned for spiritual enlightenment. It was a clear example of "the blind leading the blind." As a result, Catholicism experienced prolonged censorship, ridicule, outcries for purification of its priesthood, and atonement. With internal rivalry, ideological dissension and lack of cohesion among the hierarchy, the two thousand-year-old institution, began to lose its immense wealth, followers and prominence. Arcane religious philosophy could not prevail against the unrelenting pressure of time demanding change.

As people around the world were confronted with an uncertain future, the entrenched factions of religion and science maintained a sober air of superiority and commitment, never considering that time was a deterrent and running out. The two opposing factions never found common ground to resolve their differences regarding creation. Man was denied the inner peace of knowing who he was, where he came from, and what his purpose in life was. This uncertainly left him vulnerable while facing the greatest monumental crisis in human history. Eventually the weight of the world's burdens would force him to his knees. Only then would he fold his hands together and look to the heavens for salvation. By this act of contrition, man would acknowledge God's supremacy, the only sublime truth that echoes from the silence of eternity.

A Turbulent World in Crisis

The uncontrollable crisis on Earth caused by man's obsession for wealth and power created a planet in turmoil. To add to his problems, the winds of war constantly loomed on the horizon. His most formidable problem was a lack of commitment for embracing God's commandments. Adding to life's distractions, man's comfort zone involved living an uninhibited existence. This superficial tradeoff for life was partially attributed to the religious establishment. Their world wide spiritual revolution for mankind at times seemed twofold in purpose. Mainly devoted to their mission of saving mankind from himself, it had a tendency to ignore God's doctrines and church protocol. Elements of the hierarchy did not always practice what they preached. At times church officialdom appeared as a two-headed dragon, one breathing fire and brimstone, the other peace and harmony. This conflicting image was most prevalent when a spiritual leader intruded into the political arena or governed a nation. This practice soiled their reputation as religious advocates for God, plus it was demeaning to their profession. There was no spiritual gain when intruding into the political quagmire. Politics was a fickle, degrading, and unrewarding forum to build faith in God. There was an insurmountable hurtle to injecting religious ideology into the management of government. Different religions have varying beliefs and theologies. When they clash, the rise of civilization suffers. Political agendas impair people's judgment by confusing their reasoning and leaving them indecisive. Political messages were sometimes unreliable, distorted, intrusive, or downright untruthful. Political ideology favored either liberal or conservative views. If there is one word that pinpoints man's inability to cope with his overburdened society, it is "moderation." The lack of it downgraded every avenue of human endeavor in government, politics, religion, science, industry, and education in man's excesses. Both liberals and conservatives had a tendency to be reckless and excessive in their approach to life's problems, rarely seeking a middle ground. The obvious conclusion was that man could not keep a lid on his excesses, resulting in a world boiling over and out of control.

The lessons of history confirm that human beings require restraint when advocating political, economic, or environmental freefall. Most elected officials were charged with protecting the public's interests. They did so with one eye on their interests and the other on self preservation. This conflict between personal and political interests left them open to the corruptive influences of special interests. This unethical procedure left the public with a deep distrust and revulsion for dysfunctional government.

There were many conflicting elements in human society, some beneficial, others disruptive. In the case of religion, their strength was not derived exclusively from the pulpit. Rather, it stemmed from the efforts of faith-based initiatives. Dedicated people of all walks of life worked and served the people by administering to the poor, hungry, ill, poverty stricken, homeless, and disenfranchised. This was the uncelebrated side of religion that inspired hope and faith for the downtrodden. These unselfish and dedicated people served the world's underprivileged, and not with condescending words that sometimes rang hollow. They were the unrecognized saviors of humanity.

Through the ages, the one unanswered question that confused man's journey was, "What possessed some religious clerics to stray from their sworn mission to serve God, save humanity, and keep peace on Earth?" In the latter part of the twentieth century, the world was threatened by extreme elements of the second largest religion on Earth. In the religious world, Islam was a name given to faith preached by the prophet Mohammed in the year AD 600. He believed that he was sent to warn and guide the masses to worship one god, Allah. Those who adopted his teachings were known as Muslims, and the Islamic faith became one of the oldest and most respected religions on Earth. It grew out of war and conquest and created an empire stretching from northern Spain to India. By the twenty-first century the Muslim populations numbered fifteen billion people living in one hundred fifty countries, with scattered enclaves in other countries. In depth studies of the Islamic world revealed that the majority of these countries were progressive socially and economically and were an intricate part of the world order. The study also found that predominately Arab countries lagged behind in tolerance for other religions and retained strict and dominate control over their people. Their cloistered societies put them out of step with more advanced nations.

Religious clerical rule of a nation was extremely rare by the twentieth century. A past history of intolerance, abuse, discrimination, and deprivation of personal liberties was reminiscent of medievalism. Most progressive countries had outlawed religious interference in national affairs. In the twenty-first century, the Islamic religion gave rise to a malignant and destructive faction in their hierarchy. Cleric extremism incited and unleashed a reign of terror that rivaled the barbaric atrocities of the middle ages. The basis and excuse for their orgy of bloodshed was a passage in their holy Koran. It prohibited violence only if threatened by an aggressor. By distorting its message and intent, the clerics used it as a tool to call for a jihad (a holy war) against the "infidel," which was anyone who did not believe as they did. There was one devious and glaring flaw in the Islam clerics' mindset: they could not distinguish between an aggressor and personal ambition. There is no war that is "holy," as God would not advocate violating the sanctity of life. Behind the Islamic extremists' war was a firm belief that there was only room for one religion. Death to the infidel!

Combatants in the holy war had one outstanding feature that distinguished their activities: it was ancient tradition for women to wear veiled clothing, and men were heavily bearded and wore headscarves to hide their identity, thus preventing recognition. They were a shadow army who committed unforgivable offenses against humanity and their God. Because the fanatical clerics did not personally participate in the bloodletting, they required surrogates to wage war. This necessity gave rise to an organization called al-Qaeda. As they could not finance war on a large scale, they chose a more devious method to wage war. Secretive in their operational activities, they established underground cells in the Mideast, Europe, and Africa and eventually in the Western hemisphere. At first these small groups targeted hotels, foreign embassies that housed foreign nationals, and military troops. Because these incidents were isolated, the world did not view them as a global threat. As they grew in intensity, nations revised their appraisals, and there became a clear call for war against the terrorists. As their activities spread to regional conflicts, the Islamic leaders selected countries with weak, ineffectual governments ruled primary by tribal chiefs and warlords. These predominately Muslin countries were fertile grounds to recruit, train, and conduct their murderous activities. To recruit the young of their religion, they used the oldest tool known to mankind, mind control. This form of ideological brainwashing was so successful, the recruits became disoriented and their judgment warped. This revived primitive instincts that were traceable to his animal ancestry.

The most disturbing aspect of radical Islam is that supposed "men of God" dragged an age-old, respected religion into the muck and slime of depravity. Besides al-Qaeda, whose terrorist war was more global, a regional conflict led by Islamic militants—known as the Taliban—sprang up in a predominately Muslin nation to overthrow their government and impose strict Islamic laws. This country was also the training ground for al-Qaeda, the sponsor of global terror. Under a unified command, nations dispatched military forces to curtail their murderous activities. The holy war was not confined to killing the infidel but men, women, and children of their own faith, if it served their purpose. The crux of the matter was a conflict that could not be won by military might.

Throughout history, wars instigated by religious zealots took a horrendous toll on human life but end as an exercise in futility. A poisonous snake cannot inject its venom if headless. The Islamic extremists who injected their intolerance and venomous hatred against mankind should have been excommunicated by Islamic officialdom. By not purifying their ranks, the credibility and future of their faith was at stake. The indifference from the rank and file lasted ten long years. Finally the hierarchy realized their religion had taken the brunt of worldwide condemnation for a minority faction of fanatical clerics. The turning point occurred when Islamic nations took matters into their own hands, passing laws forbidding radical Mullahs (Muslim men) to educate their children with hatemongering ideology. This purged their ranks, but not before the military alliance between al-Qaeda and the Taliban began to unravel. The world, sick of the unending bloodshed, unleashed massive air and ground strikes, saturation bombings, and large ground forces. New technology in avionics produced unmanned drones designed to fly, and search out and destroy ground targets by remote control. They took a toll, eliminating top terrorist leaders. Overwhelmed, outgunned, and disorganized, they fled for their lives, taking refuge in underground caves and bunkers. In desperation they used their women and children as human shields to prevent air attacks. Many noncombatants died needlessly. There was no refuge for these untutored ghosts of the past. Their time had come and gone, hunted down and relentlessly destroyed without mercy. The Taliban's decision to abandon their alliance with al-Qaeda deprived them a base of operations. Consequently, the lesser militants began prolonged negotiations with the enemy government. As a result they became a minority faction in the ruling government. Former combatants disarmed and blended back into the country's population. A few diehard terrorist leaders fled to Africa with hopes of establishing a new base of operations. It was a final act of desperation. Lack of funding and resources, and in a continent racked with civil wars, their cause evaporated to become only a bad memory.

The world's reaction and backlash from the ten-year Islamic war was one of ambivalence. The conflict left a dark bloody stain on the faith's place in history. It would be remembered as a struggle for religious power. Within the religion's clerics a transition from extremism to moderation occurred, and the world breathed a sigh of relief. There was a lesson to be gained from the jihadist war. Power-hungry Mullahs still engaged in preaching intolerant and distorted ideologies of the past could not tolerate an open society. To permit their followers' membership in the modern world would be suicidal.

The revitalization of the religion's hierarchy brought a new age of hope, understanding, civility, openness, and religious tolerance. The disenfranchised terrorists became the discards of humanity without misgivings or a show of conscience for their brutal war on the infidel. In retrospect there was a combined lesson in history and Darwinism for military planners. Winning wars and upgrading cultures requires hundreds of years to evolve; it does not happen overnight. The one demoniac curse of the Islamic holy war was the actions of the deposed clerics who had inspired the war with their hate-tainted preaching. They had the privilege of hiding safely behind mosque walls. They should have been tried before world courts for crimes against humanity. However, their punishment was assured, because they had the wrath of their god to contend with. By the year 2012 some of the world's most prominent religions were subjected to constant scrutiny as spiritual advocates for God. Discontent and disillusionment with their immoral and undisciplined actions questioned their commitment to serve humanity. The Islamic war, the Catholic Church's pedophile scandal, encouragement of the reproductive process (which led to overpopulating Earth), and even Christian clergy attempting to enter the political arena all contributed toward painting a picture of religion's deteriorating purity and placed their profession on trial. The jury was the people of Earth and the judge was God.

The other religions that had sat idly by during the war still preached spiritual messages to the faithful, based on ancient scriptures. Their major innovations were concentrated on improving their centers of worship and gathering converts. The sermonizing of contemporary religion was confined to the four walls of community churches. This was necessary with commercialization of their faith. Their main attractions were more comfort, protection from the elements, and better acoustics, but above all, a haven to find spiritual enlightenment. This confined setting was an abrupt departure from the sermons God's only son preached from natural outdoor settings. They contained the embodiment of the father for all to behold in wonder and devotion. In this environment the populace found a kindred relationship with their creator. Even today as people seek a respite from the harsh realities of everyday living, they choose places of solitude and beauty, where they sense God's presence.

In biblical times there were no sound amplifiers to increase the volume and intensity of the messages that Jesus Christ spoke from the mount to his followers. His sermonizing resonated around the world. The clarity penetrated deep into people's consciousness with a promise of peace, contentment, and salvation. The message from Jesus was, "Believe in my father and you shall have everlasting life." This was the sound of rolling thunder and electric shock that woke man. For the first time in his long, tedious journey through the evolutionary corridors, he experienced hope and spiritual security knowing he was not alone. He had finally found the one answer to the question that had evaded him since birth. It was man's spiritual revelation. The son of God was living proof of God's divinity. Through his son's promise God had extended his hand to mankind. Human beings only had to take it to experience the most profound and fulfilling experience in their lifetime, a natural bond of affection between one's self and his creator. The relationship would heal the wounds of the heart, body, and soul and sooth the conscience. The revelation that man could bridge time with God as his companion was a homing beacon illuminating the darkness of eternity, his manifest destiny.

In spite of religion's efforts to refer God's sacraments to the masses, there were those who lived with impunity beyond his reach. This unscrupulous and greedy segment of Earth's society became the main threat to its survival. Their unhampered lust for power and wealth undermined the very fabric of civilization. The evolution of man did not endow him with a moral compass. It only became evident with intellectual maturity. He was then forced to choose right from wrong, good from evil. A standard compass pointed to the four cardinal directions. Man's compass pointed to the four qualities that were the signature of his species: morality, decency, responsibility, and devotion to his creator. These qualities were lacking in the selfish individuals whose only goal in life was to amass wealth and power regardless of the consequences.

As nations grew and prospered, they developed financial systems—called money or currency—based on a rate of exchange. Each country printed its own money. It provided a means to purchase and sell products as well as to service them. Money also financed the workings of government. It became the barometer that determined a person's status in life. The obsession for wealth was the root of all evil, a false illusion with bitter future consequences. Biblical scriptures clearly stipulate that man cannot serve two masters. God or money, you love one or the other. It was dehumanizing that the rich could only read the denomination of their currency and not God's word.

The composition of Earth's population consisted of three levels of wealth: rich, middle class, and poor. Mankind was incapable of addressing or reconciling the three into one fruitful society. For every step forward, he took two steps backward and ignored the disparity. It was a no-win situation for equality among the classes. To associate the word human to God's chosen life form was a stretch of the imagination. The inequity between the rich and poor was an ongoing travesty. The gap widened with every passing year. The division between the two was most evident in industrial and financial management. Top corporate officials were granted huge salaries, bonuses, stock options, and severance pay. Their compensation ranged into the millions, and they were better paid than heads of government. This rewarding situation occurred even when their employees' jobs were being outsourced to foreign countries with lower labor costs. This accomplished several rewards, including more profit, less accountability, and inferior products and shifted the companies' pollution problems to another part of the globe. Corporate mentality justified these moves claiming the world had become a global marketplace, ignoring the fact that it had already been, and long before profits declined. It was an unsavory disguise for declaring that greed had become a worldwide sickness. When profits declined, large corporations had little allegiance to their home countries, let alone the employees who had made their company successful. Their only priority was a favorable blue line on yearly profit statements. To maintain corporate wealth and power, companies employed legions of lobbyists. These human leeches attached themselves to any politician who could influence legislation that would favor their industry. In return, politicians were rewarded with large contributions to their election campaigns. Buying favors became standard practice with one hand feeding the other, undermining the core principals of free democratic government. Political favoritism fueled corporate empowerment. As a result, public voting became a mockery, creating an unwavering disgust for dysfunctional government. After retirement from political life, some politicians became lobbyists. They used cronyism and knowledge of the political system to feather the nests of their sponsors. There was a decided hypocrisy to this practice. Lobbyists wore their country's flag in their lapels, adding insult to injury.

For mankind, life in general was always being contested under duress. The incredible rise of civilization was not accomplished without paying a high price through moral decay. As the world became immersed in social, political, and economic trauma, there was a breakdown in government's will to solve the mounting global emergency. The governments and private sector's efforts to eliminate greenhouse emissions were conducted at a snail's pace and fifty years too late. Nations' industries and transportation practices still continued to dump pollution into the atmosphere. Most nations had signed and adopted treaties to control climate change, protect biodiversity, eliminate hunger and poverty, and prevent diseases. Even then, ten million children died each year from hunger, poverty, disease, polluted water, and total despair. Overpopulating the planet filled every nook of livable land. The masses lived in a depressing twilight stupor day after day, running on a treadmill of anxiety and fear. Tomorrow never came and the future became a mirage. Life was a journey through an endless tunnel, and man could not see beyond the entrance. There were no miracles, and man buckled under the pressures of an overburdened world, a planet saddled with resource depletion and a lack of renewable energy, an imbalance in world trade, and a meltdown of global economies. The more affluent segment of society began searching for more favorable living areas to preserve their lifestyles. Unfortunately, with global overpopulation there was no sanctuary to be found. To add to the swelling population, wildlife analysts predicted that by the year 2012, 70 percent of the planet's wildlife would be crowded out and become extinct. This would be a major disaster, because man alone could not survive as the only life form on Earth.

In his headlong rush and zeal to build a great civilization, man overestimated his ability to deal with the consequences. The cost of living in an overburdened and bloated society was overwhelming. It affected every facet of human endeavor, including energy use, food, clothing, and consumer purchases, and education. Governments were forced to maintain large standing armies, because man had not learned to coexist with his neighbor. Painful analysis revealed a world in over its head, a result of man's infatuation with wealth and self-inflicted excesses.

Confronting these debilitating problems caused enormous stress on his mental reserves. Many people could not cope with the constant stress. Recognizing the scope of the problem, the pharmaceutical industry developed many types of drugs to deal with the issues. They were designed to treat illness, subdue pain and suffering, reduce mental stress, plus improve bodily functions. In most cases these drugs were effective and beneficial to mankind. At times some of these drugs reacted with others with harmful results. It was clear that humans could not exist without medical assistance, and they lived in an overmedicated society.

Man's dependence on drugs did not end with treating illness. In the twenty-first century a drug-related culture surfaced, devastating mankind. The threat was more prevalent in developed nations. The drugs created an illusionary world for the addict and did incredulous damage to people's health and mental wellbeing. Those who could not cope with responsibility and personal stress resorted to taking mind-altering drugs. These addictive substances shut down the mind and body of the addict, causing them to live in a world of illusion, divorced from reality. It soon became obvious that people could not handle the problems caused by a bloated civilization. Drugs were the easy way out. The addicts' loved ones suffered a high price, watching helplessly the deterioration of one of their own. The combination of drugs and handgun availability turned the city neighborhoods into war zones. The results were overflowing prisons, drained resources, and unenforceable criminal activity. The drug traffickers were low income, impoverished, disenfranchised, and uneducated members of society. Also related to the drug culture was the smoking of cigarettes. A product manufactured from tobacco and laced with controlled amounts of nicotine—highly addictive and one of the deadliest substances on Earth. Its use brought misery, suffering, shortened life spans, and death to thousands each year. Despite packaging that clearly stated smoking this product could be harmful to your health, people still temped fate by providing a false illusion of invincibility. They and their loved ones, who watched the addict's inevitable demise, were the real victims.

This practice confirmed Darwin's belief in the survival of the fittest, where he once stated, "Let the strongest live and the weakest die" in regard to evolution. As successive generations of humans appeared on Earth, they inhabited a world in confusion. The crush of civilization had drastically changed people's lifestyles. Constant pressure from a burgeoning economy brought a complete indifference to the value of money and a lack of restraint in its purchasing power. The old conservative and moderate age of living was abandoned, giving way to a new generation of free-spending liberals. People were obsessed with materialistic values and living well beyond their means, and this new fast-track segment of society ushered in an era of false security with mountains of credit card debt and personal bankruptcy. This appalling situation caused a breach of respect between the elderly and younger generations. Elders recoiled in shock and disbelief. Even though they had lived through global recession and wars, their period was considered the "good old days." The obvious reason for their dissatisfaction with the younger set was their indifference to responsibility and their deteriorating morality. Older generations had never experienced declining morality, credit card debt, a polluted atmosphere, runaway crime, drugs, and sexual exploitation. To the elderly, the world had turned into a decadent society, rushing headlong into self destruction. Most did not recognize the place of their birth. Over time the winds of change had drastically transformed a moderately paced society into a highly pressurized and complicated world. The rate of change was so rapid, people could no longer walk through life; they were forced to run, just to keep pace with progress. Technology advanced so rapidly that new products were obsolete before introduction to the public. The elderly could only reflect and wonder: when the younger generations reached an advanced age, how proud would they be of their good old days?

In the physical and mental development of the human life form was an abnormality that appeared over time. The normal aftermath of the reproductive process was not cast in stone. Some individuals' gender and sexual orientation were not guaranteed at birth. They changed gender by transsexual surgery or adopted same sex marriages, which was contrary to the laws of nature. Those who aspired to same sex relationships were entitled to their lifestyles, but not if it jeopardized the progression of life on Earth. The definition of marriage, according to the laws of nature and God's rules of engagement, specifies that marriage is a union between a man and a woman. Without this opposite sexual union, there can be no reproduction of the human species. Over time, if a drastic increase in same-sex marriages occurred, the evolutionary process would end and it would spell extinction for the human race.

There was also a decided contrast between humans and other life forms in their approach to survival. Most wildlife lived a carefree existence except for the threat of predators. They had no debilitating problems or pressures from the crush of civilization. In stark contrast, man was forced to exist in an unrealistic, fabricated, and demoralized society. Constantly buffeted with assaults on his mental capabilities, which he was incapable of resolving, his mental progression had not kept pace with the rise of civilization. He was only able to process one problem at a time. This self-inflicted stress had a sobering effect on his decision making. The crushing weight of mental fatigue reduced his ability to become a sound and intelligent custodian of his planet. This unsubstantial rupture of man's mental capacity amounted to a decline in his evolutionary progress. Although he preferred to paint a nontransparent gloss over his shortcomings, a state of mental strain eroded the very fabric of everyone's lives. The plight of people living on Earth was obviously a critical issue in the twentieth century.

The most serious threat to their survival was attributed to public indifference. The crisis was appalling to some and irreverent to others, but there was one fact that could not be disputed: time was not on man's side, only his creator's. It did not condone intolerance or indecision. Unfortunately, the preponderance of humanity lived in a house of mirrors. The only image visible was their own reflection, and had they looked deeper into the mirror of life they would have beheld their creator with outstretched arms offering eternal salvation. For mankind the future of his species and planet were at stake. Man was at a turning point in his epic journey on Earth. His future depended on selecting one of two courses. One was to continue self serving practices; the other was to adjust his mental outlook and actions in favor of God's mandates. There was no question which direction he must take. After all, a leap of faith is more rewarding than a leap into oblivion.

The "Silentocene"

The unforgivable legacy of the terrorist war was the senseless toll on human lives fueled by overzealous and power-hungry faction of the Islamic faith. Another futility of this conflict was diversion of the world's attention from the threat of global warming. Consigned to a matter of irrelevance, this unresolved issue had taken its toll, wasting ten years of concentrated efforts to eliminate greenhouse emissions. In the meantime, the warming trend had intensified. The world was besieged with unseasonable weather and natural disasters; only a few isolated scientists related these conditions to global warming. As climate abnormalities had repeatedly occurred in the past, no one became unduly alarmed. Still behind global frustration, there was a nagging doubt whether the warming condition had a human footprint. At first, as worldwide temperatures increased, climatologists and environmentalists became alarmed. They sounded a global probe to confirm its validity and cause. Eventually, as all the scientific evidence was processed and verified, a disconcerting picture emerged. Earth scientists issued a stern warning that the planet was experiencing the advanced stages of global warming. Neither governments nor the public were convinced, but in the scientific community it raised deep concern. What could harm a centuries-old planet that had not happened many times before? Time does not accommodate short memories. Global warming began more than two hundred years ago, with the industrial revolution. It continued unabated and grew to its present level. This desperate condition was not the first crisis that had provoked public and scientific concern. Earlier atmospheric pollution was caused by the release of corrosive solutions of sulfuric acids into the atmosphere. When discharged from coal-burning plants, these acids became airborne, were carried aloft for hundreds of miles, and fell back to Earth as acid rain. These toxic acids had a corrosive, devastating effect on forests, ponds, lakes, rocks, and metal objects. Coal producers were forced to eliminate this condition by burning low sulfur coals and then passing the exhausts through scrubbers that captured the sulfuric dioxide. There was also mercury emissions from burning coal, which, when falling back to Earth built up hazardous mercury levels in many types of fish, making them unsafe for human consumption.

In later years another manmade contaminate threatened the world's environment. This contamination originated from two prime sources: industrial plants and various methods of transportation used by the public. This time the culprit was the burning of fossil fuels. When released into the atmosphere, they caused global warming. A main source was the car industry. Every gallon of gas consumed generated twenty pounds of CO_2 greenhouse emissions. Considering the total number of cars worldwide, this unchecked problem was a recipe for disaster. In one decade alone, manufacturing industries poured 360 million tons of pure carbon dioxide into the atmosphere. Such huge amounts of this odorless gas tended to warm up the planet, holding in the sun's radiation that normally escaped back into space. Over time the eight miles of atmosphere surrounding Earth could become saturated with manmade pollutants.

Besides these various sources of contamination, there was another major contributor to global warming. Earth's tropical rainforests lay on both sides of the equator and were the planet's ecological jewels. They were huge storehouses for sequestering large amounts of carbon. The rainforests were considered the most unequaled features on Earth. The sun at noon can be seen directly overhead twice in one year. This condition never occurs anywhere but in the tropics.

Equatorial climates have no winters and experience the most rainfall of any place on Earth.

As the world was faced with rising energy costs on oil and natural gas, the economic squeeze forced nations to find alternate sources of energy, a crash program that should have taken place during the past century. One of the new sources of energy were biofuels, grown from farm crops, corn, and soybeans. This started a stampede to obtain and grow a cash crop suitable to put in gas tanks. It translated into higher prices on grain-related products and reduced food surpluses for needy countries.

Because of the pressure from overpopulation and economic necessity, tropical nations began an orgy of clearing vast tracts of rainforests. The results were alarming as trees and vegetation absorbed carbon out of the atmosphere. When they died or were burned, it recycled back into the atmosphere, contributing to CO_2 overload. This slash-and-burn method was employed to convert their forest sanctuaries into land suitable for farming and raising cattle. The participants in this ill-conceived project were subsistent farmers, loggers, cattlemen, and government officials who had no regard for long-term consequences. This indiscriminate loss of tropical reserves altered the landscape, turning it into vast seas of grass that stretched to the horizon. Large portions of this newly acquired land were used to grow crops and raise cattle. Corn and sugarcane were converted into ethanol. Soybeans were distilled into biodiesel fuels. Regardless of global food shortages, nations' first priority was to fill gas tanks instead of hungry stomachs. This misguided policy further lessened food reserves for underdeveloped nations. It raised the death rate to ten million people each year dying from malnutrition and starvation. Although the farmers received the brunt of people's anger and frustration, the blame rested primarily on governments' ill-conceived energy programs and misdirected priorities. The normal supply and demand for food became a luxury the farming community could not supply, which caused the unthinkable to happen. Mankind experienced the same fear and hardship as other life forms when their food chain was disrupted.

The acquisition of new farmland also required large amounts of fertilizer to enrich nutrient-starved soil. Acid rain flushed the excess into waterways, accelerating aquatic growth and causing cancerous lesions on fish. The eventual loss of topsoil from wind erosion left only unproductive farmlands. The only success story in developing alternate energy sources was in the growing and use of sugarcane. It was far greener than corn ethanol or soybean biofuels. By 2008 carbon emissions from tropical deforestation accounted for 20 percent of the planet's total pollution. Mankind's priority to rely on fossil fuels as a sustainable energy source was a disaster in the making. Even the most mentally deficient person realized these resources were not renewable. Nations not only had difficulty managing the planet's resources, they could not reconcile the fact that the environment and evolutionary process were entwined. The impact of global warming disrupted the chain of life on Earth. Especially affected was the world's wildlife, which was forced to change breeding times and foraging and migration patterns formed over centuries. It also brought variations in growth and genetic continuity of emerging new life forms. Wildlife tells time by the length of the day and changing seasons. Their survival mechanisms were most prominent in colder regions of Earth. Its history revealed a long pattern of intermittent climate change but never at this unprecedented pace. When evolution could not keep up with prolonged weather abnormalities, it spelled crisis for life on Earth.

Ignoring the need for renewable alternate energy sources, governments at first ignored growing anger and frustration, but the prolonged stalemate over whether to burn fossil fuels left the public bewildered. The shame of the fuel crisis was that governments ignored natural and renewable energy sources, such as solar, wind, and sea that were free for the taking. Eventually, countries began to direct their efforts and money into creating vast panel arrays and towering fans to capture the wind and sun's radiation for energy. The cost of converting them to power grids was astronomical. They eventually became a secondary source incapable of supplying large amounts of energy. The only adequate source was nuclear power. In this, field development lagged behind because of the public's fear of human or equipment failure that would cause radiation leaks. The most creative minds in the scientific community had the capabilities to recycle spent nuclear fuel rods, which no country wanted, to sequester underground, a controlled procedure that would eventually reduce its mass 95 percent and increase the radioactive lifetime 98 percent. The world could not dig or drill its way out of the global energy crisis. The ecological damage caused by accidental spills from tankers and offshore oil rigs should have stopped drilling in environmentally sensitive areas. Here again, the need for fossil fuels and the wealth it generated overrode any call for global sanity. The desperate need to reassess energy programs rested squarely on the public exerting pressure to force unresponsive governments to action.

There were other secondary areas of responsibility where governments and the private sector worked in concert to solve global problems. Many countries with large farming communities worked with scientists to increase crop yields and reduce fertilizer use and pesticide overuse. It initiated programs to improve water productivity and promote conservation efforts that reduced soil erosion and carbon release. Many of these initiatives were successful and helped underdeveloped countries grow sufficient crops to feed their masses.

The scope of these efforts also helped reduce greenhouse emissions. Lagging behind in the conservation effort was industrial and transportation carbon releases, which continued to increase at an alarming rate. The ecological and telltale indicators appeared in remote regions of Earth, well away from public scrutiny. The arctic was warming twice as fast than any place on Earth. The massive ice dome on the top of the world was shrinking at an alarming rate. With warming climate, wild birds native to the southern latitudes were now seen in the arctic. The floating ice that acted as a barrier protecting the mainland from wind and water erosion gradually disappeared. This left receding shorelines and coastal flooding. In normal years temperatures in northern latitudes remain below freezing eight months of the year. The subsurface of the arctic tundra covers 20 percent of the North American continent and remains permanently frozen year-round. With warming, the upper levels of permafrost began to thaw. As a result, the moisture-laden soil began to thaw and produce new growth and dwarf trees after thousands of years of absence. In remote seas, acidification accelerated faster than any other time in sixty-five million years, releasing vast amounts of methane gas into the atmosphere. The subsea permafrost had lost its ability to be an impermeable cap. Methane was twenty-five times more potent than carbon dioxide emissions.

Melting surface tundra and huge landfills also contributed to the release of methane. This condition had never been considered detrimental to climate change. Scientists unnerved by the condition were at a loss for answers. In Siberia, the bodies of extinct wooly mammoths frozen in the ice for thousands of years reappeared. This warning indicator alone should have galvanized world opinion in favor of global warming. Earthquake intensity caused cataclysmic volcano eruptions. Some were so devastating they brought about a minor shift of the planet's axis, making it spin slightly faster. With disappearing sea ice, polar bears and seals lost their frozen environment and were forced to migrate to the mainland to survive. The most astonishing phenomenon was the reopening of the fabled Northwest Passage, which rarely accessible, was now open and safe for passage. With wide-open seas, a stampede of nations sought oil and gas drilling rights. World courts were swamped with violations of international maritime laws. It was the beginning of the arctic turf wars, an ongoing testimonial to the avaricious nature of man.

The masses were bewildered by the scientific community's indecision in forming a consensus on global warming. It rivaled their failure to resolve the four hundred year controversy over creation. Geological studies concluded that in the last two million years fluctuating weather patterns occurred at regular cycles. In the current decade, a dramatic escalation was occurring at a pace never before seen. Plant and animal life struggled to survive, and shifts in growing seasons, melting polar caps, rising sea levels, fresh water shortages, and depleted natural resources were overwhelming. They were all fluid examples of global warming. Man was oblivious to the consequences. As the scientific establishment experienced a meltdown, their conflicting research data and turf wars exposed unethical practices, errors, omissions, and distortions. International agencies were in complete denial and complicit in accountability. The major contributor to the rise of civilization was incapable of slaying the greenhouse monster it had created. To even contemplate its existence was painfully embarrassing.

It was an established geological fact that the nineteenth century's small ice age was preceeded by a medieval warming period. This should have triggered advance warning signals. The underlying source of global warming was the long-term temperature exerted by the twenty-mile-thick crust of Earth. This surface mantle was subjected to a combination of two heat sources. The first was external trapped heat from the sun, which was unable to escape back into space, and the second was internal thermal output. If not contained, the condition would have a detrimental effect on planet ecology. A confused and disenchanted public finally caved in to stress, making the threat of global warming a non-issue. This negativity would precipitate the most cataclysmic disaster the world had ever known.

At the same time the arctic ice was melting, similar conditions were occurring in the Antarctic. Large islands of ice six hundred feet wide and two hundred miles long were separated from the central mass. Scientists who study icebergs knew that they can float for years before evaporating to be recycled as precipitation. These floating masses only show 1/8 of their total bulk; the rest is below sea level, hidden from view. Floating icebergs displace water; melted ice water raises ocean levels. The sudden increase in sea levels caused oceans to break their boundaries and flood low-lying coastal areas. In the resulting panic, people were forced to flee inland to higher ground. This population displacement caused massive relocations, famine, disease, inadequate housing, and a reduction in human services. The global ratio between salt and fresh water distribution was a key to man's survival. Sixty-nine percent of the planet's fresh water was frozen in ice sheets, snow, glaciers, and wetlands, and 30.1 percent lay beneath the ground in aqua filters collected from rainwater.

Undrinkable saltwater was converted to fresh water by desalination plants, introduced in1970. Over the years scientists experimented with three methods of conversion. All were costly and inadequate to supply the world with fresh water. Consequently, 3.3 million people died each year from water-related health problems. As the water-deprived masses around the world increased, people began to collect rainwater and snow in any container available. The shortage of water forced farmers to abandon millions of acres of tillable land. Agriculture slowly began to decline, resulting in food shortages. The development of large megalopolises sealed off large areas of land. Asphalt and concrete prevented rainwater from re-supplying underground water tables. Draining into waterways, it caused reservoir levels to decline. Because of long-lasting droughts, utilities lost their capacity to generate hydroelectric power. Electric grids went offline, blanketing whole regions in total darkness. The period between sunset and sunrise became one of dread and depression. The candles and oil lamps of the colonial period returned and acted as a substitute for electrical power. As power failed, space monitors still functioned to produce photo imaging, but without functional receptors they became useless. Ground stations that gathered weather changes for the military, farmers, and the general public became inoperable. Even the giant Hubble telescope, deployed 353 miles above Earth in 1970 became inoperable. Countries that shared the international space station were forced to shut down and recall their astronauts. When the telescope and orbiting surveillance equipment were abandoned, the world lost its eyes in space.

As climate reversal prevailed around the world, the die was cast. The most intelligent life form on Earth was incapable of preventing ecological disaster. Scientific discoveries and advances had occurred rapidly in the twentieth century, but finding new energy sources was a slow process. After two hundred years of unrestrained contamination, the condition could not be resolved with short-term solutions. It required long-term commitment from every sector of the planet—government, private industry, and the public sector—to create a universal plan to stop the irresponsible madness crippling the planet. Nations had to unite and mobilize the best scientists to begin a crash program similar to the 1940 Manhattan project, which produced atomic energy. If science could land a man on the moon, surely they could launch a mission to save the planet. They were responsible for creating the crisis, so who better to resolve it? As the urgency of an impending disaster loomed, extreme conservation methods were universally implemented to conserve water and electricity. As water supplies dwindled, nations built giant heat convectors capable of melting polar ice. They were dispatched to the Arctic and Antarctic to melt and reclaim fresh water. As these portable convectors melted ice, the water was transferred into seagoing tankers and then transported back to the world's thirsty populace. The project helped but could not keep pace with the demand, and eventually the polar icecaps were depleted.

With unrestrained atmospheric contamination, global warming side effects were felt around the world. It finally prompted automakers and industry polluters to implement crash programs to eliminate carbon dioxide emissions. The delayed action was fifty years too late, for the crisis had grown to unacceptable proportions. The punishing effects of the disaster were felt around the world. Shortages of food and water, and deplorable living conditions and healthcare all contributed to human misery. Nations with overstrained budgets eventually became insolvent. The unwelcome situation demoralized the public, creating havoc. By his own indefensible actions, man was now on the verge of becoming an endangered species. The greenhouse problem was not the only cause of public concerns. Along with upper atmospheric pollution, the eight-mile layer of atmosphere surrounding Earth was being saturated with particulates, microscopic bits of solid or liquid released as a byproduct of burning fuel or other substances. They had a harmful effect on the human heart and respiratory system, especially in the elderly.

Another disturbing condition at the turn of the twentieth century was the doubling of Earth's population every thirty years. Man had sown his seed indiscriminately, with little regard for overpopulating his planet. When medical science increased man's life expectancy, the birth rate exceeded the death rate. The swelling population explosion caused staggering problems such as fewer ways to dispose of human waste and raw sewage, navigating polluted waterways, handling garbage and trash incineration or finding new ways to bury it, and the release of large amounts of methane gas into the atmosphere. The population explosion only intensified the need for more housing and land for farming. Eventually, as Earth's natural ecosystems absorbed additional foreign matter, the upper atmosphere became oversaturated. Then the pollutants began to contaminate the oxygen levels needed for survival. At sunset, western skies turned blood red.

In spite of the dramatic changes in climate and people's lifestyles, worldwide response for a unified formula to resolve the crisis was sporadic and hindered by special interests wanting to preserve their wealthy status. The scientific focus on the warming problem centered wholly on the branches of Earth sciences, geology, geophysics, and geomorphology, which dealt with the land and subterranean relief features of Earth. The planet man had inherited was considerably vulnerable to long-term extreme temperature changes from external and internal sources. The most formidable effect was the pressure on tectonic plates. Mounting heat caused plate disruption of plate alignment. The up or down movement of tectonic plates had a devastating effect on the planet's geographical features. Under internal pressure, hot magma is forced up through volcanic conduits. The resulting lava flows enlarge land masses and sea bottoms. Under riding plates thrust up mountains and change river courses. Their flowing currents deposited huge amounts of silt, enlarging coastal shorelines. Wind, water, and ice constantly eroded surface features. Geotectonic interaction and plate disbursement had been ravaging the planet since its birth, but never at the intensity as during the twentieth century. Mega earthquakes and increased volcanic eruptions spewed huge amounts of ash over large regions of Earth, shutting down commercial airlines, resulting in a huge loss of profits.

Erratic climate and environmental fluctuations were normal side effects of a stable ecological system. Constant warming upset the fragile ecological balance that stabilized the planet. The stark reality of the mounting disaster was that the masses were caught in a mighty vise, squeezed between two unrelenting heat sources, and there was no escape. The scope of the threat touched every living thing on Earth. Scientists estimated that the earth's outer crust was only twenty miles thick, Which by any gauge is a delicate piece of real estate. Lying beneath the crust was the mantle zone, eighteen hundred miles thick. Beneath this was the outer core consisting of molten magma. This underlies the inner core thought to be solid nickel and iron. Constant heat from one front was volatile under normal circumstances, but with unending heat from two sources it was a lethal injection, disrupting the planet's ecological system. It brought raging floods, long droughts, water shortages, hurricanes, tornadoes, and mega earthquakes. Although seismographic stations around the world monitored the wave intensity of earthquakes, little attention was devoted to monitoring temperature fluxional changes in the earth's crust. Considering the planet's history of intermittent ice ages, this indifference was inexcusable. The earth's low tolerance for extended heat or cold was confirmed by past studies on extracted deep sea and glacier cores to determine glacier frequency. As stated, ice ages were not new to Earth, but they were to the populace. Over past epochs of antiquity, the planet had experienced several ice ages. Each one lasted ninety thousand thousand years, followed by inter glacier periods lasting twelve thousand years with moderate temperatures. Their predetermined appearance was caused by a change in the tilt of the earth's rotation during its elliptical path around the sun. This condition reduced the sun's radiation, causing the planet's crust to cool. Global warming broke the cycle of global play back long before its due date.

Very few in the scientific establishment associated global warming with increased natural disasters. The debate over rising temperatures ran the gauntlet of speculation but produced no final consensus. For the scientific world, their inability to pinpoint the cause of the warming disaster was the ultimate failure of their profession, a milestone in their efforts to create a thriving civilization on Earth. Continually searching for answers to the warming trend, perhaps there should have been an admission of guilt for causing the crisis in the first place.

Despite the pros and cons of the warming threat, it grew each year. Public apathy, government inaction, and money-driven industries all contributed to the crisis. Also, the lack of international agreement and support didn't help the situation. The cost of curing the disease overrode the cost of the disease itself. The scientific community was in complete disarray, unable to put a human fingerprint to the warming trend. It eventually became clear that those responsible for verifying global warming were more interested in protecting their bank accounts, propagandizing and influence peddling for those who would benefit. When the day of reckoning finally arrived, they would pay the ultimate price.

Perhaps the most disturbing factor was that those who had effected global warming were incapable of slaying the monster they had created. As all efforts failed, a hazy shroud formed over various regions of Earth. It was most evident over major cities, industrial complexes, and higher elevations. The depressing grayish veil partially blocked out the blue skies for days on end, fluctuating with temperature change—denser with warm conditions and waning with cooler temperatures. Seen from space, the once-spellbinding blue-white colors were now faded and somber in appearance. This lackluster vision of Earth resembled a giant revolving mirror, reflecting the sun's radiant heat back into space. For mankind and his planet, this was the ecological tipping point. The belt of greenery that had encircled the equator for thousands of years had disappeared, leaving the planet mostly free of green zones. The earth had destroyed 75 percent of its forests and in the process lost its heat retention. The planet was now in crisis mode. Geothermal heat from the earth's interior could not supplement the loss of radiant heat from the sun. Without heat retention, the earth's crust began to cool. It brought a reoccurrence of early ice age conditions.

At first, atmospheric temperatures remained unchanged, but on Earth a different condition emerged. As the planet's crust cooled, sea ice that had disappeared reappeared in the Arctic and Antarctic. The newly formed ice sheets began to regain their former mass and expand. With cooler temperatures, other normal conditions prevailed around the earth. With more favorable temperatures, the populace breathed a sigh of relief, but their reprieve was short lived. Temperatures did not stabilize at normal levels and continued to decline. This forced scientists to reassess their predictions for the planet's stability. As it steadily grew colder, climatologists pushed the panic button and announced that the planet was facing the possibility of a new ice age. Shock and panic reverberated around the world. As temperatures continued to drop, nations issued proclamations to calm the public's fears and deal with the crisis. Clothing manufacturers labored twenty-four hours a day to meet the demand for insulated garments. Lower temperatures reduced growing seasons, bringing soaring prices. Varying degrees of inadequate and excessive rainfall caused intermittent droughts and extensive flooding.

As the coldness intensified, birds and animals were the first to change breeding and feeding habits. The nostalgic sounds of migrating geese occurred much earlier in the fall. The global weather changes caused surface winds and ocean currents that drove the Gulf Stream to change wildly over land and sea. Bewildered climatologists were incapable of predicting reliable weather forecasts. Earth was ravished by increased volcanic eruptions, wildfires, floods, typhoons, hurricanes, earthquakes, and unseasonable tornadoes.

As the planet stood poised for impending disaster, who was responsible for the crisis? The world's scientific community was directly responsible for the impending tragedy. Building a thriving civilization whose foundations was based on materialism and a corrupting dependence on acquiring wealth was a pure indictment of irresponsibility. Even wasting centuries on enhancing their professional image by gathering physical evidence to support unlimited theories was all to no avail. Their greatest failure was in not realizing that beliefs and faith were crucial to human survival.

The solution to their self-defeating labors rested squarely on the relationship between God and time. The latter had no binding covenant with science. As the crisis grew, the masses demanded scapegoats for the global irresponsibility. Accusations and recriminations abounded, and world jurists became vigilantes bent on revenge. When the gavel came down, the soothsayers and scientists who had misread the evidence and misled the world became the focus of public anger, a final indication that incompetence and irresponsibility had its price. As nations collapsed from within, they lost their national sovereignties along with spheres of interest. The world's monetary systems became insolvent and inviable. Money, bonds, and securities became worthless and were burned as fire starters to keep warm. People's wealth deposited in banks became worthless, and banks closed their doors. Domestic products and services were no longer available, and industrial plants stopped production. People lost their infatuation with wealth and material things as the instinct for survival became the main issue.

In remote and colder climates sea ice appeared and slowly spread outward. The mechanisms of sun and ocean currents began to exert less influence on weather conditions. Aquatic life, deprived of full sunlight, began to die. Plankton, krill, and other food sources maintained undersea disappeared. The giant whale, leviathan of the deep, disappeared, their underwater antics and resonating harmonics no longer gracing the world's oceans. As underwater life slowly died, some floated to the surface but eventually sank to the bottom and became part of the fossil record. Dying sea life turned the ocean floor into a watery graveyard.

On a worldwide scale the abnormal coldness caused less recycling of warm moisture from the equatorial zone. Maritime air masses still moved northward from equatorial waters. Their collision with colder air still produced rain, which fell in milder regions, but in more northern latitudes it fell as sleet and snow.

As the planet's ecological systems collapsed, religion and science, in a show of solidarity, joined in the race for survival. Neither confessed their complicity in the great debate that had kept the world in denial for four hundred years. The threat of a new ice age had a long-overdue impact on humanity. For the first time in man's history the masses united into one coherent society. Racial and religious bigotry disappeared as people came together in universal brotherhood. It was the end of an era. Tragedy united the rich and poor and eliminated racial and religious intolerance. The days of lavish spending and plush living came to an abrupt end as the rich joined the poor. Although the long overdue blending of humanity came at a late date, it was the final vindication of the human race. In the world courts, those valiant individuals who had pleaded for restraint and environmental sanctity were eulogized, but the gesture was only symbolic. There was no death penalty, only recriminations for the irresponsible people in government and private industry who had looked the other way and put their planet in jeopardy.

Around the world, intense growing coldness brought drastic changes to the planet's geological appearance. The two icecaps at opposite ends of the Earth began to regain their former mass. The size and weight of the surface ice grew. Normally, melt water from glaciers flows back into world oceans. This replenishing flow slowly decreased into a trickle and then stopped completely. The scene that followed was right out of the Pleistocene epoch. With so much of the world's moisture imprisoned in continental glaciers, sea levels eventually began to drop, reaching an amazing four hundred fifty feet, twice the depth of previous ice ages. In coastal regions, people stood helplessly by as ocean, bay, and inland waterways slowly drained away in what amounted to a permanent ebb tide. High watermarks on piers and jetties served as moot reminders of the calamity facing the world. Tidal marshes, bays, and inlets drained away, exposing barren ground. Coastal shorelines now extended ninety miles at sea to continental shelves. Ancient ghostly shipwrecks appeared, and manmade junk reefs and imperishable debris from ships littered the sea floor.

As ocean levels declined for the first time in ten thousand years, land bridges appeared between continents. The newly exposed sea floors were covered with decaying marine vegetation and sea life. The odor, combined with salty sea air left a lingering stench that burned the nostrils. With declining sea levels, desalination plants no longer had the product availability to convert saltwater to fresh. As major seaports became inoperable, commercial fishing boats and cruise liners lay abandoned, their rusting hulls forming huge ship graveyards.

Another casualty of the waning seas was the pleasure boat industry, with small boats stacked high in abandoned marinas. Without seaports, the tankers that had transported oil and water were beached. Town, city and country streets were lined with abandoned cars, trucks, busses, and every kind of mechanized vehicle. The weapons and munitions manufacturers were the first to close their doors. Storage warehouses, depots, and military armories were all saddled with unused equipment. Silos with unused ballistic missiles were disarmed and their facilities abandoned. They stood as a silent testimonial to man's indifference to the sanctity of life. The world's fear of nuclear annihilation was the end of an era. Former military bases were converted into huge dumps for discarded hardware, tanks, artillery, and weapons. Airport runways were lined with abandoned aircraft of all sizes, and they ranged into the thousands. As the skies became silent, man no longer looked up. His eyes downcast, he now saw a world that resembled a scorched earth, a devastated landscape, the result of approaching armies invading their country. Only this time the enemy would appear from the north, and its weapon would be the icy threat of a bone-chilling death.

The first life forms to sense climate abnormalities where the wildlife. Birds and animals were quick to sense weather changes. Survival mechanisms that had evolved over millions of years made adjustments to meet any condition. As the world's tapestry of green foliage ceased budding, trees and shrubs withered and died. Their foliage had been the key to survival, capturing the sun's heat and preventing its return to space. Bare branches extended heavenward like grotesque spears. The changing seasons that had brought spring, summer, and fall was replaced by twelve months of winter. Birdsong that had mellowed the hearts of people ceased, followed by an unearthly silence that spread across the land. Birds perching on barren limbs, now without a food source starved, and with pitiful chirps toppled to the ground to become food for carrion hunters. Wild animals starved, their pitiful wails filling the night air with protest.

As the coldness increased the death toll rose to the millions. The scene was one of complete demoralization. Without hope, the 2030 doomsday capsule became the ultimate choice for people to experience a painless demise, and mass suicides accounted for most of the deaths. Prisoners were all released back into society, their fate no longer in question. The multitude of human lives lost was the final tragedy to the story of man. The military, with no earthly mission or purpose, became each nation's burial squads. Unending mass graves dotted the countryside, most interred without markers. Crematories burned twenty-four hours a day, and body ash accumulated in huge piles. Even with the stench of burning bodies, people huddled around these facilities to keep warm. As the bitter cold refrigerated the planet, people took desperate measures, stripping all combustible materials from homes, farms, businesses, landscapes, and industrial plants. The acid smell of wood smoke constantly permeated the night air. This telling odor and lack of food and water brought a complete meltdown of human resolve.

In normal interglacial periods, ice movement of the mass is one mile in twenty-two years, or 235 feet per year. Because white ice has no insulating effects, it tends to create colder conditions. White surfaces do not soak up heat; they bounce the sun's heat back into space. The people of Earth should have observed the frozen icecaps at each end of the earth as a constant reminder of the planet's deadly past. The constant buildup of glacial ice upset the stability of the mass. After ten thousand years of dormancy, continental glaciers began to move, slowly at first but accelerating as new falling snow provided a slick runway for the ice to glide over. These giant mountains of frozen water produced their own weather systems because of the intense cold. Their chilling output refrigerated everything for more than one hundred miles in its path. No physical barrier could withstand the tremendous pressure of a moving glacier. In some northern regions their height loomed two miles above the surface. Eventually these monstrous walls of blue-white ice began to serge ahead at the rate of 123 yards per day, or six miles in three months. In some areas, with little obstruction, they galloped along at the incredible rate of three miles in eight days. The massive juggernaut promised death and destruction for everything in its path, pushing ahead into valleys, covering ponds, lakes, streams, and rivers, even riding up hills to envelop mountain summits, sometimes slicing off their peaks. The glaciers' leading edge, hardened by accumulated rock, had the destructive force of a giant bulldozer, gouging deep furors in rock formations. As it pushed southward, the crushing momentum snapped off trees, rendering them into matchsticks.

In desperation, the world's masses began migrating, fleeing to escape the onslaught of ice. As they fled south, their numbers grew fewer and their passage was marked by unending snow-covered graves. No matter how far or fast they traveled, a wall of ice in close pursuit loomed on the northern horizon. There was no escape; it was a race against the inevitable. Finally the numbing cold and lack of food brought total despair and with it the human spirit died, believing God had forsaken them. On his own insistence, man had now become the hunted instead of the hunter. Around the world, devastation was complete and no region on the planet escaped the cold, threatening menace.

Even the world's oceans were not immune to the destructive impact. Lashed by turbulent seas, massive columns of ice broke loose from glaciers, falling into the ocean, and they appeared as floating islands drifting into tropical waters. Intense cold lowered ocean temperatures, and they took on an opaque appearance. In the atmosphere, pollutants acted as a filter and less sunlight reached Earth. Consequently, the planet lost 75 percent of its color spectrum. Sunlight had provided depth perception, distinction, and shadows. The colorless landscape forced mankind to live in a simulated state of color blindness. Mountains lost their towering image, the valleys their depth. Forest glens were without shadows and deserts no longer exhibited shimmering mirages. Salt marshes, sandy beaches, and oceans lost their silvery patina. As Earth's beauty faded before people's eyes, they finally realized what was occurring. God's embellished light on Earth was being extinguished. In those terrifying days man's world faded into obscurity. He was subjected to the futility of absolute despair. Life became meaningless, and his spirit collapsed from within.

As the migrating ice edged its way southward, it leveled towns and smashed into major cities. Towering sky scrapers were dislodged from their foundations and sent crashing to the ground. Cities became mountains of rubble carried miles from their original location. The towering ice mass resembled a white piece of earthmoving equipment, gouging out dirt and rocks and carrying them out to sea. As the icy tentacles reached the oceans, they spread out to form sea ice. This again created slick runways for the advancing ice mass to glide over. Their icy fingers reached out to engulf offshore islands. It was the beginning of glacier dominance and the takeover of the world's oceans, an event never before experienced by man. The massive weight of the ice depressed Earth's crust, forcing tectonic plates into the molten interior. Dormant volcanoes became active and new ones appeared, along with old fault lines. New crevices opened up beneath the sea, causing bubbling torrents of steam to cloud ocean floors. On the surface, giant whirlpools swirled like the water in a bathtub going down the drain. Earth reacted violently to the massive convulsions. Scientists had long known that volcano dust carried aloft could blacken out the sun, preventing its heat from reaching Earth. This condition, combined with the loss of heat retention, accelerated the growing coldness. The smothering effect of tectonic plates released billowing clouds of pumice and deadly gas into the lower atmosphere. Surface ice and the sky took on a dirty gray appearance. This unsettling condition brought worldwide depression and prayers to God for salvation. It soon became clear that the creator could not or would not undue what mortals had done.

As the world died around man, his most depressing experience was the deafening silence. With civilization coming to an end, men, women, and children became disoriented and lost unto themselves. Harassed by the constant numbing cold, it penetrated their very souls. At this late date, man finally realized that time was not on his side. By his own indefensible actions, he had become an endangered species. In the long correlation of Earth's history, epochs in time had ranged over astronomical periods. In sharp contrast, his lifespan was now a mere thirty-five years. In resignation, scientists named this new age "Silentocene," the Age of Silence.

In the end, all traces of the earth's surface and civilization disappeared beneath a solid white mantle of ice. The two converging ice sheets collided just below the equator. The crushing massive weight of the northern glacier overrode its southern counterpart, thrusting up a mountain of ice that girdled the planet. From space, Earth appeared as a giant revolving snowball with a constricting belt around its midsection, squeezing out the planet's last ounce of breath. It would take eight hundred years to cleanse itself and return to a normal pollutant-free atmosphere. Perhaps God in his infinite wisdom would permit some form of life to reappear. The planet eight thousand miles in diameter at the equator resembled an icy cocoon. Beneath the frozen canopy were the remains of man's civilization. All flora and nine hundred million life forms perished, along with nine billion human beings.

Dominating the world stage, man's final curtain call was an unassuming but poetic performance. He walked onstage with an air of resignation, offered no apology, bowed slightly with the hint of a smile, turned without a word, and disappeared behind the curtain. His time had come and gone. An unearthly silence followed as the human dynasty on Earth came to an end.

The providence of man and his demise had no simple explanation. God's unprecedented departure from traditional creation to introduce a special life form had one handicap. Man was required to achieve his manifest destiny on his own cognizance. That responsibility was his Achilles' heel. So outstanding a beast, so magnificent as a human being—what went wrong? With the magnitude of problems stemming from his bloated and overburdened civilization, man could not cope with the mental overload on his faculties or manage his planet. Eventually he lost his way and the mutual covenant between God and man became tarnished and frayed, all because of his irresponsible actions. His life story was like reading a controversial book, always subjected to critique and review. His inevitable end was a monumental tragedy, for God had lost of one million years of creation, all in vain. The sad irony of his demise was that while standing at death's doorstep, he was still asking, "Who am I, where did I come from, and what was my role and purpose in life?" There is little more to be said of man. The inscription on his gravestone reads, "Here lies a human being, a life form without a moral compass."

The Ending

In these last desperate moments, as I dwell on my terminal situation, I am overwhelmed with a deep sense of guilt and remorse. There is no consolation in knowing that I, like many others, was negligent in preventing the demise of our planet. The constant drone of our nuclear facility has ceased, and when the backup systems shut down, I will be at the mercy of the encroaching wall of ice. I fully realize that my end is near because of the deep chill that permeates my living quarters. Before me in the light of my flashlight is a DD 2030 capsule, and I know what I must do. My one regret, at this late date, is that I must face death alone.

Outside the facility looms the menacing wall of ice. The giant heat convectors have become silent. They act as a silent reminder of the futility of our manmade civilization. Eventually the menacing ice wall will engulf our facility. The night sky is full moonlight, exhibiting endless interacting oddities of the color spectrum. If the scene was not so deadly it would be considered beautiful. Strangely enough, something is occurring. The shrieking winds and ice reverberations have ceased, and there is an unearthly silence. What is happening? Now a brilliant light is radiating down on the ice summit. I cannot believe what I am seeing. Spotlighted in its brilliance stands the figure of a man. He is dressed in a flowing alabaster robe and his arms are outstretched toward me. Am I dreaming or hallucinating?

He beckons to me. Is this a miracle? Every nerve in my body is alive in anticipation. What is going to happen? In the brilliant light his countenance is like no other I have ever seen. It is timeless, seemingly etched in marble. All the deep emotions humans experience are reflected, yet it is one of complete peace and serenity. It cannot be; he is speaking and although I cannot hear his voice, every word penetrates my inner conscience.

"Fear not, for I am Jesus Christ, the son of God. I am living proof that in my father's house, life is eternal. Because you are the last of your kind to return his love and devotion, I was sent to receive you. More than two millennia ago, I walked among your people, and in my heart was the seed of my father's love and salvation for mankind. Those multitudes who accepted his divinity unto themselves where granted the gift of eternal life. Those who rejected his affections were confined to the silence and obscurity of eternity without recourse. The precious gift of life you humans shared was not confined to Earth. His creative search for perfection encompasses the entire universe. Many worlds and forms of life exist beyond the stars. His one foremost desire was the need for recognition of his divinity. Without that acknowledgement, his efforts were meaningless and without purpose. Accepting the father offered your people the opportunity to know eternal life. With all the multitudes of life God created, you humans were his most cherished creation. He invested centuries of time, waiting for you to achieve perfection but was unable to prevent your headlong rush to self destruction. It was the father's fervent wish that humans cast in his image would become emissaries and take his message of salvation and everlasting life to the heart of the universe. Unfortunately, mankind's journey through time is now ending. Your people have reached the sunset of your lives. The father has never forsaken you even though humans could not fulfill their destiny. The accomplishments during your stay on Earth must be admired but not commended. I did not return to Earth to accuse or admonish you for the many offenses against humanity. That course is for the father to judge. I was sent as his surrogate to escort you to your final salvation. The human experience is only the beginning of a wondrous journey through time, one in which the father will grant you immortality.

"Someday when the earth is purified there will be a sequel to the memory of mankind. God will release his icy hold on your world, and there will be a renewal of life. Come to me, my son; heaven awaits you. God has granted you the ultimate reward of an afterlife. This precious moment will be one of transition. The peace and contentment that evaded your earthly life now awaits you in God's embrace."